THE KILTED GROOM

A Scottish Romance

LAUREN SMITH

ISBN:978-1-967219-99-5 (e-book edition)

ISBN: 978-1-967219-00-1 (print edition)

FOREWORD

Hello my lovely readers!

Thank you so much for diving into *The Kilted Groom*! This novella was a delightful, emotional story that captured my heart! It was previously part of a set of stories grouped around the theme of an antique ring.

Naturally I had to work in some history (one my passions), and my love for Scotland. I hope you all enjoy this story! I plan to write more stories in the future involving weddings and Scotland as a theme, so please be sure to sign up for newsletter (which is linked at the end) and to follow me on the social media links provided at the end as well so you don't miss any news!

CHAPTER 1

This is insane.

Ainsley Hazelwood's headlights could barely eke out anything on the black rain-soaked road. The deluge that had swept over her car in the last hour made it impossible to see past the sharp glints of rain on her windshield. She'd left Glasgow hours ago, and she swore the storm had followed her.

She gripped the steering wheel tighter as she glanced at the GPS on her rental car before returning her eyes to the road ... or where the road used to be. She couldn't distinguish between the side gulleys and the center pavement any longer, even with her high beams on. Driving through Scotland in the middle of the night without a clue where she was going was completely *insane*. The address for the bed-and-breakfast she was trying to find still didn't show up on the digital map. All she could do was set the address for the village of Greystone and hope she'd get close enough to locate the inn.

Rain sluiced down the windshield as the storm deepened. The dirt road, which was once solid, turned into mud … mud that was trapping her car. The vehicle slowed—and no matter how hard she pressed the gas pedal, the car only inched along. A few dreadful moments later, it stopped; the car rocking backward as it settled deep into the mud.

Ainsley curled her fingers tight around the steering wheel as a wave of grief and frustration hit her out of nowhere. She pressed the hazard-lights button on her dashboard, wishing she could do something, anything else instead of cry, which was very much what she wanted to do if she didn't find a way out of this mess.

"I don't even want to be here," she breathed in the dark, and lowered her head until it pressed into the steering wheel. Hot tears leaked out of her tightly closed eyes, and she choked on a sob.

The only reason she was here was that her grandmother, Agatha, the woman who had raised her, had died and left behind a small fortune—with strings attached. Ainsley was supposed to return an old ring to a family in Scotland. The ring had been in her family since 1917, but Ainsley hadn't learned about it until her grandmother had passed away. She glared at her purse, which held the little blue velvet box containing the antique ring. She wanted to throw it out the window, forget why she was here, and just go home. But returning that ring to Scotland had been her grandmother's last wish, and she couldn't turn that down.

"Gran, I need you," Ainsley whispered as she lifted her head and wiped her tears away with shaking hands.

She shouldn't be falling apart like this. She was twenty-eight, a grownup for God's sake. But grief had a way of taking her back to when she was a child, reminding her how much it hurt to lose those she loved.

She glanced again at her purse, which held not only the antique ring but more importantly, the letter her grandmother had written to her. Ainsley had read it so many times in the last week, she'd memorized it. Parts of her grandmother's words came back to her, almost as if the woman's spirit was here in the car.

I know you will miss me terribly, but we both know it was time for me to go. You will feel alone, but you aren't. You have a great talent for making friends wherever you go—which is why I must ask you to do this one thing for me. In this box, you will find a ring, a very old one. It belonged to my great-great-grandmother, Saoirse. It was to be her wedding ring... She asked for someone in our family to return the ring to Scotland so old ghosts may finally rest. It will be an adventure for you, one I believe your heart truly needs. And perhaps, when it is done, you'll discover your path in life again.

Ainsley remembered the moment she'd first seen her grandmother's words on that piece of paper. The scrawling penmanship, once so elegant and perfect, had turned slightly spidery from Gran's shaking hand as her health and strength failed her toward the end. When Ainsley had received the note and the box from her grandmother's attorney, it felt like her heart had broken all over again.

"Why did you never tell me about this?" Ainsley asked, even though she knew no one would answer. She found it strangely comforting to talk to her grandmother as though the beloved woman was still there, listening. Sometimes she swore she could still smell Gran's lilac perfume and feel the light touch of a hand upon her cheek. It made her feel insane, just like agreeing to come here when her grandmother's attorney had explained the stipulation of the ring's return to Scotland that was written into Gran's will.

Unable to resist the compulsion a moment longer, she took the ring box out of the purse and opened it. Sliding the ring onto her finger, she stared at it. The fine hairs on the back of her neck rose and she felt... A deep sense of love, followed by an unbearable sorrow, seemed to flow from the ring into her. What had this ring seen? What ages had it lived through? What hands had it graced? She wished she knew more about her family. Gran had always been quiet about things when it came to family, probably because losing her daughter, Ainsley's mother, had brought them both so much pain.

Twin dots of light appeared in the distance ahead of her, and she fought down a wave of panic mixed with relief as she realized it was another car headed her way. What if this person was a serial killer? That was nuts! The odds of that would be low, right? Her mouth formed a grim line as she watched the approaching headlights. She would either get help or get murdered at this time of night.

"I should have stayed in Cincinnati," she muttered. She could have continued her work at her PR firm, focused on her meetings the next morning. But she'd quit that job to do this ... to run away to Scotland on a mission for her dead grandmother. Her chest suddenly tightened, and it was hard to breathe. She closed her eyes for an instant, inhaling through her nose and out from her mouth, counting her breaths to calm herself.

The other vehicle, a forest-green Land Rover, stopped, facing the opposite direction on the road. The driver rolled down his window and waved his arm for her to do the same. She rolled her window down, getting a better look at the man.

"Car trouble?" a deep Scottish voice rumbled. She peered up at a shockingly handsome man with dark brown hair and light-colored eyes. He seemed to be in his late twenties or perhaps his early thirties, and his dark hair, slightly long, fell into his eyes.

"Er ... yeah. I got stuck in the mud. No all-wheel-drive, I guess," Ainsley called back over the pelting rain.

"Ahh. I see. Where are ye headed?" he asked.

"Um..." She hesitated a moment, praying this man was not a serial killer before she decided to trust him. "To the Thistle and Briar Inn? It supposed to be near Inveraray? Do you know how far that is?"

The Scottish man's eyes crinkled at the corners as he smiled. "Let me guess, the GPS didna recognize the address?"

"Exactly! It just kept telling me the general direction, but once I hit the bridge, I wasn't sure if I missed the inn or even the town."

"I ken the place, lass. I can call a truck to tow ye, but it would likely take a few hours."

She winced at the thought of spending more time stuck in the dark. It left her feeling far too vulnerable.

The man's eyes softened. "By yer accent, I ken ye

must be far from home. I lived here all my life, lass. I just left Greystone and wouldna mind taking ye back that way, if ye wish. If it'd make ye feel better, ye can even call the local police and have them on the line while I drive ye. 'Tis dark and if I was a woman, I wouldna trust a strange man."

Something about him seemed so *genuine*. She swore she almost heard her grandmother's voice whisper, *"Trust him."*

Ainsley studied the man and his expensive vehicle. Hopefully he wasn't an axe murderer or something. She decided she would trust him. She didn't want to stay here all night, waiting on a tow truck.

"Okay. I have a suitcase—"

"Not to worry," the man said. "I'll fetch it for you, lass."

The man got out of his car, and she had a chance to see that he wore a green-and-black plaid button-up shirt and jeans, which fit his legs perfectly to show off his muscles without being too tight. He leapt down into the mud without a care for his black boots.

"Will ye pop the boot for me, lass?" he called out as he approached the back of her rental car.

"Boot?" *Oh, right, the trunk.* She hit the trunk button, and the man pulled her suitcase out. It was one of those big rolling suitcases, but he carried it with ease while holding it well away from the mud. With his other hand, he opened his own trunk. He set her suitcase inside and turned back to her.

When she started to open the door and get out, he halted her with a hand.

"Wait for me," he cautioned as he approached the car and opened her door. "Ye have the rest of yer belongings?"

She grabbed her purse and her backpack and gave him a nod. He quickly took her purse and backpack and put them in his backseat, then opened the passenger door on the other side of his car before returning to her.

"Now, let me carry ye." He bent and before she could argue, he'd scooped her up in his arms. She squealed and grabbed his neck, making him chuckle. "I willna drop ye," he promised.

It was strange ... and delightful to be carried like this. She'd never had a boyfriend who'd just picked her up like she weighed nothing and carried her about. But given that this man was built like one of those sexy Highlands warriors from her favorite TV series, she shouldn't have been surprised. Take his shirt and give him a sword, and she'd swoon on the spot.

"Sorry ye're getting wet, lass," he murmured as he reached his car and set her in the passenger seat. "But I figured ye would rather be a bit wet than a bit muddy, eh?"

"Definitely," she agreed. Her green sweater was damp with rainwater, but she didn't care.

She'd brought a rain jacket, but she'd left it deep in her suitcase because she hadn't really given a thought to the weather. Now she knew she was paying for her lack of planning with frigid temperatures and downpours. The icy water soaked through her sweater and jeans until she was shaking from that damp, chilly weight of it.

Her rescuer locked her rental car and then returned

to his own vehicle. As he climbed into the driver seat, he handed her a thick, green woolen blanket that had been sitting folded up over the center console between the two front seats.

"Put this on yer lap." Then he cranked the heat on the car and turned her seat heater on. "The inn is only a few miles from here," he murmured as he turned around to face the way he'd come.

"Th—thank you," she stammered through chattering teeth. She shot a glance at him, completely awestruck that he seemed unaffected by the cold. In the glow of the instrument lights, she was able to make out the wet hair falling into his eyes and the crystalline drops of rain that clung like diamonds to his dark lashes. His jaw was square, his nose straight, and his lips full. He was, quite simply, *gorgeous*. Heat radiated off of him in a way that made her realize just how cold she felt ... and *lonely*. She had dated on and off the last ten years, but she never really felt lonely until now, until her grandmother had passed away. She was the last of the Hazelwoods, with no siblings, no cousins, no aunts or uncles.

Ainsley shivered, unsure if the cause was the rain or a longing to belong somewhere again—or perhaps a mixture of both.

"You'll be fine, lass," the man murmured. "We'll get to the Thistle and get some hot stew down you and put ye to bed." He shot her a quick, charming grin as he said this.

The way he said *put ye to bed* sent a wave of welcome and mortifying heat into her face. Fortunately, the darkened car hid her blush.

"Thank you. Seriously. I don't know what I'd have done if I had to spend the night in my car." His scent drifted to her as the heater warmed the air around them. He smelled like rain and old forests, the kind she wouldn't mind getting lost in. She'd always liked the aroma of cedar and pine mixed with a hint of something masculine.

He chuckled. "No sense in doing that. Ye'd have a sore back on the morrow."

He shot a glance her way. "I'm Leith Creighton." He held out a hand and she shook it. Faint calluses covered his fingers and palms, and the hint of roughness to his skin made her body tingle in feminine awareness.

"Ainsley Hazelwood."

"'Tis a pleasure, Ainsley," Leith replied. "So, what brings ye to Scotland?"

"Sightseeing, sort of. I've never really been outside of the U.S. except for a trip to Mexico once." She didn't tell him about the ring; it felt too secret, too personal.

"Well, Scotland is verra different from Mexico." He chuckled again, and the rich sound warmed her all over. It made her think of scotch pouring over ice in a glass, the dark amber and richness of it completely enticing. Her grandfather had died when she was fourteen, but he used to drink scotch on Sunday nights and read a good mystery novel while she and Gran cooked together in the kitchen. The old memory made her chest suddenly tight with a sharp, unexpected pain. She made a little sound, and fought off the wave of emotions that threatened to pour out of her.

"Lass? Are ye all right?" Leith pulled the car off the road and put it in park as he faced her.

God, this is so embarrassing. She didn't want to cry in front of a stranger, especially one who conjured up her favorite fantasies.

"There now," he soothed as he put a hand on her shoulder. "What's the matter, love?" She brushed the tears from her eyes and tried to turn away, but he caught her chin and turned her back to face him.

"My ... my grandmother died recently and sometimes I just..." Words failed her.

"Ah," he tutted softly. "Yer heart is broken. I ken that pain, lass. Cry if it will make ye feel better. Tears are nothing to be ashamed of. They honor the ones we love."

She struggled to control herself, and only when she felt her body cease its trembling did Leigh pull the car back onto the road and start driving again.

"We arna far," he said as he pointed to a faintly glowing gold set of lights in the distance.

"I hope they won't mind me being so late," Ainsley murmured.

"Mr. Fife, the Thistle's owner, willna mind. He stays up late, and his wife is up early. Between the two of them, they see to the guests."

"You know them?"

He nodded. "I live nearby. I was on my way home from the little village, Greystone, where yer inn is."

"I'm so glad you came my way," Ainsley said, and she meant it.

"'Tis no problem to help a lady." He flashed her that

grin again, the one that would have made her knees buckle if she'd been standing. Maybe it was the close confines of his car, or the way she could smell rain, a hint of forests and a scent that seemed to be uniquely his, but she felt bewitched by this stranger.

When they reached the little village of Greystone, Ainsley glimpsed the shapes of the adorable cottages and little shops in the darkness. They were half illuminated by lamps shining with welcome in the cold, rainy night.

Leith parked in front of a two-story structure made of white stone and timber. A sign painted in brilliant colors and gold lettering said, "The Thistle and Briar Inn."

"Ye should go on inside. I'll grab yer bags and join ye."

"Oh really, I can get them—"

Leith met her gaze with an amused and utterly masculine look. "Nonsense, lass. Let me do this for ye."

"All right, thank you, Mr. Creighton."

He shot her a bemused glanced. "Please, call me Leith, lass."

"All right ... Leith." It felt way too intimate to use his name, but she liked saying it.

"Now go on inside." He nodded at the inn.

She grabbed her purse and rushed through the rain to the entry door.

Warmth engulfed her when she stepped inside the inn, a fire lit in the fireplace of the nearly empty main room. Four small tables with wingback chairs filled the center of the room, and a pair of chairs bracketed the fireplace. Two older men sat in chairs by the fire. One puffed on a pipe and shot her a curious look before turning back to the conversation with his companion.

"Evening, miss," a man in his late sixties said. He stood behind the bar counter wearing a dark green waist apron embroidered with white thistles. He was cleaning glasses in the sink as she walked over to the bar.

"Hi," Ainsley greeted him. "I'm Ainsley Hazelwood. I have a reservation for three nights."

The man's eyes brightened. "Ahh, Ms. Hazelwood. I was wondering when ye'd turn up."

"I'm so sorry for being late. My flight was delayed, then my rental car got stuck in the mud and—" The front door opened behind her, and the man behind the counter scowled at whoever entered.

"I dinna want yer kind here, get out!" he barked at Leith, who had just set her bags down by the door.

Ainsley's entire body tightened with tension at the sudden animosity in the room.

"Ach, hush, old man." Leith grinned as he walked over, and the barman suddenly chuckled and held out a hand to Leith, who shook it.

"Ye left and now yer back, eh, laddie?"

The sudden tension Ainsley felt faded as she realized the barman was only teasing Leith.

"Aye. I found this bonnie lass stranded on the road." He nodded at Ainsley.

The barman held out a hand to her. "I'm Paul Fife, Miss Hazelwood."

"Call me Ainsley, please." She shook the innkeeper's hand. Leigh's warmth radiated just behind her, feeling wonderful and comforting in a way she didn't want to examine too closely.

"Do ye want to go on up to bed? I can show ye to yer room," Paul offered.

"Ach," Leith growled. "Can't ye see she's half drowned, Paul? Why dinna ye let her get out of her wet clothes, and then warm her up some of Molly's stew, eh?" Leith suggested. "I would like some too, in fact." He patted his stomach, which Ainsley guessed was flat based on the trim outline of his button-up shirt. Ainsley found herself smiling at Leith's charm as he verbally sparred with the innkeeper.

Paul only laughed. "All right, laddie. I was about to offer that to her myself, young pup. 'Tis too cold outside to go to bed with an empty stomach for either of ye. Here's yer key, Miss Hazelwood. Leith will show ye to your room, 'tis number four. I'll have your stew ready when ye come down."

She accepted the key from Paul. The heavy, old brass key had a lovely tag hanging from it with a scripted room number written on it.

"You don't need to show me to my room," she said to Leith as she faced him. His damp clothes clung to him in a way that should have been illegal for the thoughts it sent spinning in her mind. Her heart kicked a beat as she resisted the urge to brush the rain-slicked hair out of his green eyes.

"Let me carry yer bags, lass," he said softly. There was something so seductively sweet about his words, about the way he asked, that her heart clenched in warning as if to say, "Do not fall in love with this man."

Because she *could* fall in love with him.

Her hand moved toward his, giving him the key before she could think better of it.

With an almost bashful grin, Leith led the way up to her room. The stairs were carpeted with an old, thick, red plaid pattern, and her soggy shoes sank into each step, making the old wood beneath creak. She tried to keep her eyes off Leith's ass, but it looked so good hugged in those jeans he wore.

They didn't speak to one another, but the silence was a comfort in and of itself. She needed time to gather her thoughts. Leigh paused before a room with a brass number four on it and used the key to open it. As he opened the door, she had a sudden, silly daydream that she and this man were going to share this room, that they were together, a couple... And oh wow, the fierce longing she felt for that to be true was startling. But this man wasn't hers, and they weren't together.

Stop daydreaming, she silently chastised herself.

"I'll grab yer bags." He was gone an instant later, letting Ainsley look around the little room.

The queen bed had a red coverlet and white sheets. A pair of deer antlers hung above the bed, and green curtains framed the window that looked out over the street. There was no TV, only an old clock on the nightstand. Ainsley had stepped into an unplugged world, and it felt comforting. Her skin was so cold and her toes felt like ice, but as she looked at the fluffy bed that would keep her cozy when she pulled the covers back in a short while, she knew she would sleep better tonight than she had since Gran died.

"The room all right?"

She turned to see Leith's tall form filling the doorway as he set her bags down.

"Yes, it's cozy. I love it," she admitted honestly.

"'Tis a bit old-fashioned, I suppose, but it's always looked like this." Leith's smile was soft, his gaze distant as though flashing through sunny memories. "Paul and Molly inherited the inn from her father and kept things this way. No fancy TVs or any other modern amenities."

"That's okay with me. Honestly, it looks perfect. I just want to fall into that bed and—" She halted as their gazes met and the gentleness in his face turned suddenly hot, searingly hot as though speaking about beds had lit him up inside.

He cleared his throat, his voice a little deeper. "Why dinna ye change and come down for stew." He brushed his wet hair out of his eyes as he looked at her.

"What about you? You're soaking wet," she blurted out.

"Dinna worry about me, lass; I'm used to being cold. I work in the fields." He grinned, revealing a hint of a dimple in one cheek. Damn, the man was too handsome. His rich green eyes sparkled with what she decided to call Scottish mischief.

"I'll be downstairs waiting for ye." He closed the door behind him.

Ainsley lifted her suitcase up onto the luggage stand and opened it. She dug around until she found fresh jeans, clean shoes and socks, as well as her favorite thick cable-knit cream sweater. Once she'd changed, she felt a little more like herself again. She lingered in the room a minute longer, wondering if Leith had meant anything more when he said he'd wait for her. It had been a while since she'd dated, and she'd gotten rusty on reading men. Maybe he was just being nice? Everyone in Scotland so far had been really nice to her.

But still... He could have been flirting. Would it be so bad if she flirted back a little?

She brushed the tangles out of her hair before she went downstairs to be enveloped in the aroma of a hearty stew. As she reached the common room, she held back in the shadows for just a moment, feeling like she was in-between two worlds. She studied Leith's form as he sat at one of the tables by the fire. Two bowls of stew sat steaming in front of him. He and Paul were teasing each other, and Ainsley drew in a slow breath, marveling at how perfect it felt to be here in this moment. How could she feel so welcome in a place so far from home?

I'm here, Gran. I'm here, she thought before she stepped into the light and toward the gorgeous Scotsman who waited for her.

CHAPTER 2

Leith Creighton glanced away from the bar when the American woman came down the stairs. She had combed her hair and it caught the light now, gleaming like polished wood. She looked far better than she had a few minutes ago. Her eyes were still red and a little puffy from crying, but damned if she wasn't more beautiful *because* she'd shown her vulnerability to him.

Ainsley Hazelwood. He let her name linger on his tongue, liking the way it felt. He'd been on his way home when he'd seen her car lights on the road and was damned glad he'd stopped to see if she was all right. Sometimes they had flooding or minor mudslides from the nearby mountains.

"Feeling better?" he asked Ainsley as he stood and pulled back a chair for her to join him. The two older men who'd been here had vacated the chairs while Ainsley had been changing her clothes, and Leith had pulled the chairs up to the table to help warm the woman that he rescued.

Her blue eyes held his as she nodded, a blush staining her cheeks. The woman was bloody adorable when embarrassed. Not that she had anything to be embarrassed about. She was in a foreign land, grieving her grandmother and had car trouble. Any decent person would have wanted to cry under just one of those circumstances, let alone all three.

"Yes, thank you. You really saved me." The smile she gave him sent an explosion of butterflies in the center of his belly. He would have helped anyone he'd come across tonight, but he was selfishly glad it was this woman, whose smile lit up the room.

Now, heat crept into his own face at her words. He just wanted to help. Any decent man would have. He liked being useful.

"'Tis no trouble. Now try this. Molly's famous beef stew." He gestured to the bowls on the table.

"It smells amazing. What's in it?" She sat down in one of the chairs and he pushed her close to the table before he sat down across from her. She drew her bowl nearer and retrieved one of the silver spoons on the table.

"Aberdeen Angus beef, onions, garlic, red currant jelly, red wine…" He paused, recalling what Paul had once told him.

"Carrots, potatoes, tomato purée, bay leaves, beef stock, Worcestershire sauce, salt and pepper." Paul finished reciting the ingredients as he came over to the table and set two glasses of water and two glasses of whisky next to them. "Drink up yer *uisge bagh* and ye shall be warm again." Paul winked at Ainsley before he turned his back to the bar.

"What did he call it?" she whispered to Leith as she lifted her glass up to study its amber contents.

"*Usige bagh*. 'Tis Gaelic for water of life. It means *whisky*. This one is Talisker from a distillery on the Isle of Skye." He lifted his glass up and inhaled the scent. "Broody, heavy peated, but balanced by a satisfactory sweetness of just a hint of brown sugar and vanilla." He took a sip. The dram tasted like heaven.

"You sound like you belong in a whisky commercial." Her bemused smile tickled him, but he only nodded at her to try it herself.

Ainsley took a sip and when her blue eyes returned to him, they were lit with a pleasure that curled through his stomach. "Oh, wow." She suddenly smiled, big and bright, and it was as though the sun had stepped out from behind the clouds.

She was a beautiful woman, Leith admitted to himself. He had been single for over a year, which felt like centuries some days. But it wasn't just a woman's body he missed; it was her companionship. His last relationship had ended amicably—his girlfriend had moved to London, and after two months of staying in touch long distance, they decided they were better as friends. Since then, he had been focused on his home and all the responsibilities that came with it. He'd had no time for dating, let alone a relationship.

Sitting by the fire, whisky warming his belly and that

beautiful smile beaming at him, he felt keenly that need to share his life with someone again.

"My grandfather loved whisky. I never tried any until now." Ainsley swirled her whisky, watching the amber liquid dance in the glass.

"Really? Ye're a whisky virgin?" The widening of her eyes and the pink in her cheeks alerted him to the implications of his word choice. He tucked away the pleasure of her blush, and carried on. "Well 'tis no better place than Scotland to have yer first taste."

Her eyes flashed with a sudden, startled heat. He hadn't realized how sexual his words had sounded, but he didn't take them back. Drinking a whisky, a good one, was like making love to a beautiful woman. It was an act not to be rushed and ought to be savored sweetly. He'd be damned if he didn't talk about whisky with the same romance in his words. Besides, he couldn't resist enjoying Ainsley's beauty, both inside and out. What harm would it cause to enjoy the evening with her?

"I never realized whisky could be so sweet," she mused.

"Aye, 'tis very sweet." His mind couldn't help drifting to the question of whether she would taste as sweet, and he had a feeling her kiss would easily rival the whisky. He needed to distract himself from such thoughts. Seducing a woman on her first night in Scotland wasn't exactly chivalrous, and he'd been raised to respect women on every level. But it didn't mean he wasn't tempted by the curve of her cheek and the flash of her eyes.

"Now try the stew," Leith encouraged. He had missed dinner tonight and was glad for a reason to come back since he'd given his house cook the night off. Molly's stews were legendary. He waited until Ainsley had taken a good bite before he tasted his own. The hearty flavors exploded on his tongue with the earthy, familiar taste that always reminded him of his child-hood. As he swallowed the stew, it warmed his entire body. Such a stew had been served on the coldest winter days, and there was nothing better than sitting before a roaring fire and eating while listening to his father tell stories. Christ, he missed those days dearly, and he missed his father and mother even more.

"My God, I could eat an entire pot of this," Ainsley said as she dug into the stew with gusto. They ate in companionable silence for several minutes, just listening to the crackling of the fire as it snapped and popped.

Leith enjoyed watching Ainsley eat. It gave him a chance to study her. He guessed she was around his own age. He was twenty-nine, but it was possible she could be a year or two younger. Her blue eyes were soft, with a hint of gray in them that made them look as deep as the sea in some moments and more mercurial at other times. Her hair was rich brown, interwoven with strands of gold and russet.

He was vastly curious as to what an American tourist would be doing here all on her own. The tiny village of Greystone didn't usually get tourists like other villages or cities in Scotland did. They might get the occasional tour bus passing through, but rarely did anyone stay. Something about her told him that she wasn't here simply to see his country. She'd been scared, frustrated, and there'd been a desperation in her eyes that was only now beginning to fade as she ate contentedly beside him. This woman needed something—he just didn't know what—but if he could help her, he would.

"So, Ainsley, tell me about yerself," Leith prompted as they enjoyed dinner by the fire.

"I'm from Ohio, near Cincinnati. I worked at a PR firm."

"Worked? Ye arna still working there?" he asked.

She shook her head. "A hedge fund bought it and started running it into the ground. The new CEO wanted me to stay, even offered me a promotion, but I wasn't interested so I left. I was hoping something would inspire me. I just haven't found what that would be yet."

"What kind of work did ye do there?

She scraped the last of her soup into her spoon and swallowed it before answering him. "I would work with companies that wanted to refresh their branding and generate public awareness of their services."

An answer suddenly clutched at Leith's mind, but he reined in his excitement. "Would ye ever work with, say, a building or a place, rather than a company?"

She sipped her whisky. "Oh yes, definitely. I've done several brandings for libraries and a few public parks. Those can be more fun than companies."

His hopes rose and he had to force himself to stay calm, lest she hear his excitement. "What about an old castle? There is one not far from here, close to the loch, and I ken the owner needs some help."

"A castle nearby?" Ainsley's eyes widened as she took another drink of her whisky.

"Aye. It was built in the 1500s. It has about forty rooms, a carriage house, and mostly functioning farmland attached. The castle is considered a Category A."

"Category A?"

"Aye, 'tis a historical designation. It limits what renovations one can do with the property, in order to protect the structure's historical significance."

"Is A the highest category?"

"Aye."

"Does it need much renovation? What do you think the owner's goals are for the property?"

"It might need a bit of renovation. Part of it was destroyed in a fire a long time ago. I ken the owner wishes to have more visitors come to the property, tourists and the like to generate some income. He might wish for ye to stay a few weeks to see the property and get a feel for the place." He searched her face for a reaction. "Would that be a problem?"

"No, not really. My apartment at home is close to my friend's, and she can collect my mail for a few extra weeks."

"Ye have no pets or a significant other who needs to be seen to?"

She shook her head, a sudden sad expression replacing her look of curiosity. "No, it's just me. Has been for a while."

"Me too," he replied just as softly.

"Oh?" And with that single syllable, uttered so gently, so full of concern for him, a stranger—she'd nearly stolen his heart.

"I've no siblings, and my parents are both gone." A

sigh escaped him at the admission. "I havena been in a real relationship in a long time. I've been busy with work."

She offered a commiserating smile. "I know what that's like. Work can stretch to fill your life if you let it." She finished her whisky and studied her empty glass. "You don't suppose Mr. Fife would mind if I had another?"

"Not at all, lass. Allow me." He took her glass, their fingers touching. A spark of awareness he had not felt in a long time, except when he'd carried her to his car tonight, tingled through his entire body at the mere brush of her skin against his. He cleared his throat and walked over to the bar. With a nod to Paul, he reached over the bar and retrieved the whisky bottle. He returned to their table and poured two more glasses, one for each of them.

"So what about you? Have you lived in this part of Scotland your whole life?" Ainsley asked as she settled deeper into the armchair and sipped her whisky.

He took a drink of his own and considered how best to answer. "I lived in Glasgow for about five years, then my mother got breast cancer. She died within a year, and my father soon after—with a broken heart, you know."

"Oh ... I'm so sorry." The genuine heartbreak in her words was a balm to the stinging memories of losing his family. The two of them were silent a long moment before she spoke again.

"Do you really believe people can die of a broken heart?" she asked, her eyes dark as midnight shadows covered her face.

He didn't answer right away, even though he knew what he would say. It was simply that the truth of his belief always caused such a deep ache.

"I do... Although I believe men are the ones who succumb more than women. Not because I think men love more deeply, but I think women find a way to shoulder their grief in a way that's different than men."

Ainsley let out a soft sigh. "I think you might be right somehow. My grandmother loved fiercely, but she didn't stop living when my grandfather died. She simply poured all of her love into everything else after he was gone. She didn't lose herself or bury herself necessarily in other things, but she kept on going as though she knew it mattered. And it did, because I needed her."

Leith leaned forward a little, more than curious about her. "Did she raise you?"

"She did. My mom had a drinking problem. She was in a hit-and-run accident and someone died. My mom couldn't live with the guilt, so she drank herself to death. I was just seven when she died."

"Christ, lass, I'm sorry. I didna mean to ask something so painful."

She shrugged one shoulder. "It was a long time ago. My dad was never really in the picture. He and my mom divorced when I was five and he has a family in California now. He doesn't want anything thing to do with me." Her fingers trembled around her whisky glass.

Leith reached out and covered her hands with his, lending her his strength, his calm, hoping it would help her.

"The man is a fool not to want to know ye," Leith murmured.

Ainsley smiled, but it was one full of pain. "Maybe," she said. "But my grandparents were there for me. I felt normal when I was with them."

Leith sighed. "I hate that we think 'normal' exists. It doesna. No one is ever really normal, no one. We shouldna want to be normal either."

She smiled through her teary eyes, and Leith was struck again by her beauty. "I'd say it's the whisky talking, but I think you really must be *this* nice," she said.

Leith smiled back at her. "I'm just a fool for a lass with pretty eyes," he said, his voice huskier than he intended it to be. Hell, if he was honest, he was a fool for any woman brave enough to bare her soul like this to him.

"Oh yeah?" Ainsley leaned a little closer. "I'm a sucker for men with green eyes."

His world seemed to expand as he fell into her beautiful gaze. To hell with resisting the temptation, he was going to kiss this woman. He leaned in—

"Leith, I'm closing up the bar," Paul called out, breaking their momentary spell. "Help yerself to whatever ye need."

"Thanks Paul," Leith replied, keeping his gaze on Ainsley. "I suppose I should stay the night. The rain is heavy," he mused. His SUV could handle the mud, but something about Ainsley made him want to stay, to take another risk entirely.

"You should *definitely* stay." She finished the last of her whisky and he reached across the table, his fingers touching hers. And once more, that strange and wondrous fire lit up beneath his skin like fireworks.

"Then I'll stay."

Ainsley was hot all over, her body burning as she asked the hot Scot to stay. She knew between the whisky and her own wild roller coaster emotions, she was acting bolder than she'd ever had in her life. But maybe that was why she was here. To do something different, to be a different version of herself. It was time to get out of her shell and do something unexpected.

"Do you think Mr. Fife would mind if we took that bottle of whisky upstairs?" she asked Leith.

His lips kicked up in a crooked, charming grin. "He wouldna, but I would. Two glasses are enough for a new whisky lover, lass."

Damn, how did this man make being a gentleman so hot? It was the sort of masculinity that women dreamed about, where the man a woman was with took care of her, watched out for her.

"Then how about I just take *you* upstairs?"

There, she'd said it. She'd put herself out there with this gorgeous green-eyed Scot. Leith's eyes were soft, but heat simmered there too.

"I'm honored, lass, but are ye certain? Ye've been through a lot."

"That's why," Ainsley said. "I think I need this. I

need you." Wow, she was just going full crazy, telling a total stranger she needed him, but in that moment she didn't regret it.

"If ye're sure." He studied her face, seeking something in her eyes that he seemed to find.

"I am." Ainsley curled her fingers around his and stood. She led him up the narrow staircase and into her room, closing the door behind him as he followed her inside. Then she turned to face him, trembling a little.

Leith gently curled his hands around her arms. "You haven't done this before, have you? Taking a stranger to yer bed, I mean."

"Is it that obvious?" She tried to laugh.

"'Tis my first time too. We doona have to do anything, Ainsley." The way he said her name more than made her toes curl.

"But I really do," she assured him. "I think if you kiss me, I'll stop being nervous."

Leith held her for a long moment, his green eyes navigating her face, searching for any sign that she didn't want this or him. Then he leaned in, his face nuzzling hers before his lips brushed against her own.

Sheer electricity shot between them and she gasped, leaning into him and grasping the lapels of his shirt to draw him closer.

"Yes," she murmured against his mouth.

"Yes," he echoed, his voice deliciously deep and slightly rough.

He smelled like rain and Scottish forests full of ancient trees and even older secrets. She kissed him, absorbing the heat of him as he moved them backward toward the closed door. He pinned her there, his tall, hard body holding hers in place as he returned the kiss. Colors burst in front of her closed eyelids and desire rushed like a swiftly flowing river through her entire body, carrying away the last of her nerves.

Leith didn't rush her. He kissed her as if he had years to learn the shape of her mouth. The taste of her. He tunneled his hand in her hair, fisting his fingers in the strands as he held her captive and deepened the kiss. His tongue traced the seam of her lips and she opened for him, reveling in the erotic way his tongue danced with hers. The whisky on their lips enriched the kiss with a smoky flavor.

"Ye taste like heaven, Ainsley." He moaned against her mouth as he pressed his hips deeper against hers.

The way he said her name made her feel dizzy, like she'd had another glass of whisky.

"So do you." She rocked against him, her body humming with need. Tomorrow she would question her decisions, but tonight this man would chase away the pain, sorrow and replace it with passion and fire. He would give her a memory that she would hold on to for the rest of her life, one night with the hot Scot. She was living a romance novel in reality. She reached up to undo the buttons at his throat, baring his golden skin.

"How are you tan in October?" she asked.

Leith lifted one of her hands and pressed soft, lingering kisses on her knuckles. "Long days by the loch in nothing but my kilt and boots."

Her eyes widened. "Nothing else? Do you mean it's

true what they say about Scots wearing nothing under their kilts?"

He let out a deep laugh that had her smiling too.

"I believe that's the whisky talking, my bonnie lass," he murmured with a lazy grin as he tipped her chin up to kiss her again. His tongue played with hers until she swore her entire body was melting.

"Hmmm." He made a sound low at the back of his throat as she finished undoing the last of his shirt buttons. Her hands slid up his muscled torso and chest, exploring him. He had a light dusting of dark hair on the center of his chest that was smooth rather than springy, and she liked it. When she circled one of his nipples with her fingertips, he dug his fingers into the bottom of her ass, gripping her possessively.

Ainsley leaned in and flicked her tongue against his nipple. His head fell back.

"Lass, yer mouth ... the things I want you to do to me with it."

She smiled before kissing her way to his other nipple. He captured her chin and forced her head back up so he could give her a rough kiss, one that made her feel owned. Because whoever belonged to this man would love every minute of it.

"My turn," he growled as he suddenly lifted her up in his arms, spun away from the door, and carried her to the bed.

She gasped as Leith dropped her on her back and positioned himself on top of her. He slid down her body until his shoulders rested in the vee of her thighs, then he pushed up her sweater. When he found the cups of her bra, he brushed teasing fingertips over her nipples, which pressed against the sheer barrier. Then, with a wicked gleam in his eye, he pinched one nipple while he kissed his way down her belly to the top of her jeans.

"I think these need to go, lass," he murmured before he unbuttoned her jeans and tugged at them. Her pants slid down to her ankles, his eyes following the fabric and her eyes watching him, her skin burning at his gaze. He chuckled as he slipped her shoes off and threw them over his shoulder, socks and jeans following, before his fiery gaze returned to her. Her face heated with awareness as she followed his gaze, and soon turned to mortification as she remembered which sensible cotton panties she'd chosen to wear that morning.

"Are those little sheep?" he asked, as he traced the little embroidered sheep on her sky-blue underwear.

"Um ... yes?" She squeaked the last word out as he playfully pulled her panties aside and eased a finger into her.

"Christ, you're tight. How long have ye been without a man, love?"

"Too long." She writhed as he moved that finger inside her, playing with her. It was wildly erotic to be half-dressed while Leigh penetrated her with his finger.

"Oh God," she whimpered as he inserted a second finger inside her, gently fucking her, rousing her body in a way it hadn't been in a long time.

"Are you going to play with me all night?" Ainsley challenged.

Leith winked at her, that dangerous dimple making a brief, flirty appearance on his cheek. "Not *all* night." He slowly withdrew his fingers and then he licked them, his eyes hot on hers as they stared at each other.

He reached for her sweater and she helped him peel it off. Then she unclasped her bra and threw it to the floor before she reached up to her waist to remove her panties. But he stopped her.

"Leave them on, for now," he ordered. Leith stretched out on top of her, his mouth claiming hers in a wild, almost untamable kiss. When she was dazed from his lips on hers, he nibbled his way down to her breasts. She cupped his head, her fingers clenching in his hair as he sucked on one nipple tenderly. His other hand shaped and kneaded her other breast in a rhythm that made her body full of a lazy, liquid heat. She'd had wonderful lovers, but Leith stood in an entirely different category. He worshiped her body in a way no one ever had before. When he moved his mouth to her other breast, she let her head fall back in dizzy pleasure.

"I want to take ye dirty, lass. I want to take ye long and slow. I want ye in a thousand ways," he whispered against her skin. "Can I have ye, lass?"

Could he have her? There was only one answer.

"Yes ... please, Leith. Yes."

As her consent escaped on a moan, the heat in his green eyes burned even brighter.

"Then I'll have ye every way I can until dawn."

Leith rolled her onto her stomach and lifted her hips up, placing a pillow under them to angle her body for him. Then he tugged her panties down to her upper thighs just below her ass. He gave each cheek a light slap which set fire to her body, and then he unzipped his pants.

"Condom," she groaned the reminder.

She heard the distinctive sound of a condom wrapper torn open and then he was entering her, pushing deep at an angle she'd never tried before. She lay prone beneath him as he knelt behind her, his knees on either side of her hips as he surged deep.

Ainsley gasped, her body singing with pleasure as he filled her. He sank to the hilt, letting her body adjust a few moments before he took her. It was a primal claiming, a desperate pounding that shattered her from the inside out with the most powerful climax she'd ever had. The second she went limp, she felt him thrust a few more times into her and groan her name before collapsing on top of her, their bodies a mess of tangled limbs soaked in sweet sweat.

"Holy shit..." she breathed. It felt like her brain had just short-circuited.

"Aye..." Leith chuckled before he kissed her cheek. "And ye're mine until dawn, lass."

CHAPTER 3

Leith woke an hour after dawn and found a beautiful, sexy, *very naked* American woman curled up beside him. Flashes of last night came back to him and his body responded, but he knew he couldn't have her, not again. Their one night was over, and he would not break his promise—even though he had this wild desire to have her forever, not just one night. He had been honest with her. He had never had a one-night stand, and now he knew why.

The idea of leaving this woman felt wrong. He wanted to stay in bed, curled up around her. and wake her with kisses as the sunlight poured over her bare skin. He didn't want to say goodbye, even though Ainsley was a stranger from another country. She was only here temporarily. He was tempted after last night to ask her for help with his home so she might stay for a little while longer, but that was a discussion for later. He needed to get her car and drive it back to the inn so she wouldn't have to walk there and do it herself.

He carefully disentangled his limbs from hers. Their clothes were strewn everywhere and as he bent to retrieve his, he spotted those adorable panties with sheep on them. Seeing those on her had made him so hard he'd had trouble getting his jeans off last night. He couldn't stop a grin as he picked up her panties and placed them atop the neatly folded pile of her clothing which he'd arranged for her. Then he searched for her purse and found the rental keys. He finished buttoning up his shirt and paused by the bed, looking down at Ainsley. Unable to resist the temptation, he pressed a kiss to her forehead and tucked the blanket up more firmly around her.

Paul and Molly were both behind the bar setting out breakfast for travelers at the inn as he came down the stairs. Paul shot him a sly grin.

"Ye didna take a spare room last night, laddie?"

"Ah... No." Leith smiled bashfully, but he said nothing more than that. "Would ye do me a favor, Paul? I want to retrieve Ms. Hazelwood's car from the road and bring it back so it will be available when she wakes up. Would ye mind coming with me and driving my car back while I drive hers?"

"Sure, Laddie." Paul kissed Molly's cheek and grabbed his coat.

They drove over the now dry roads and stopped by Ainsley's rental car. He handed Paul the keys to his Land Rover, then got into Ainsley's little Toyota sedan and drove it back to the inn behind Paul who drove Leith's SUV.

Leith parked her car in front of the inn and went back inside with Paul. He was about to go back upstairs with his cell phone buzzed.

Dougal: Repairmen are here. Need you back.

With a sigh, he set Ainsley's car keys on the counter. "Molly, I've got to run. Will ye give these to Ms. Hazelwood when she wakes up?"

"Of course." Molly took the keys and handed him a foil-wrapped meat pie before she sent him on his way.

Leith drove toward the little dirt road that ran directly toward the loch and his home, Blair House. The old medieval fortress, perched on the edge of the loch, was built of brown, craggy stones. Half of the old castles in Scotland were empty shells, ruined remnants of another age, but not Blair House. It survived Culloden and the clearances in the middle of the 1700s. His ancestors had managed to keep their lands and their home free of British rule by walking a fine line between autonomy and appeasement. He'd grown up knowing his family's legacy was tied to the castle's continued preservation. It had been a private home for his entire existence, but as labor and supply costs rose each year, Leith knew he had to consider ways for the estate to start paying for itself. Tourism was booming thanks to some Scottish Highlander show that was airing on TV. If he could find a way to put Blair House in the path of those tourists, he might find a way to preserve his home for many years to come.

He left his car in the carriage house, which had been

added to the castle in the early 1800s. It now served as a car garage for him and visitors who came to stay.

"We expected ye back last night! Dougal's meeting with the workmen for ye." Mrs. Timmons, the housekeeper and cook, said as he came through the door to the kitchens. A pot of something was brewing on the stove, likely porridge. Even though he'd eaten Molly's meat pie on the drive home, he was already hungry again.

"Morning!" He kissed the older woman's cheek. "I spent the night at Paul Fife's inn."

"What? Why?" His housekeeper demanded.

"I found a woman on the road."

"Ye found a *woman* on the road?" She dropped her large spoon in the pot of porridge and placed her hands on her hips. She stared at him as if he was speaking another language.

"Her car was stuck. Ye know that bit of mud past the little bridge into Greystone? The rain fairly turned it into a bog. The poor lass couldna move. So I gave her a ride to Paul's inn and stayed for a late supper. Since it was raining, I spent the night."

Mrs. Timmons muttered about Paul good-naturedly before she gave Leith a bowl of porridge.

"Does Dougal need me to meet him now?" he asked the housekeeper. As both the house steward and groundskeeper, Dougal was in charge of most of the upkeep and renovations. He was in his early fifties and had lived at Blair almost as long as Leith had been alive.

"No, he said when ye came home to make ye eat breakfast, and then ye can join him."

Mrs. Timmons shoved him out of the kitchens. He took his bowl to the large dining room and sat alone in a chair at the end of the table. As he ate, he faced the thing that had been secretly haunting him for the last year. He was lonely. He lived with Mrs. Timmons, Dougal, and a small staff who helped keep the place clean, but he had no family, no way to feel connected to this place. It was his home, his legacy. He couldn't just walk away, but he wanted more than a legacy to tie him here.

Leith ate his porridge and thought back to last night with Ainsley. Something about his night with Ainsley had changed him. He'd let down some of his barriers. And in the darkness of the room, sharing her bed, he'd confessed so much about his life, about what he felt he had missed, what he wanted, and how he'd change things. In turn, she'd whispered about wanting to live boldly, to stop letting fear control her.

"Fear of what?" he had asked her last night.

"The fear of failure," she had murmured against his chest.

He had stroked her hair and held her little tighter. "The only way you can fail is to never try. Trying is the opposite of failing."

She had wanted to know how he'd gotten so wise.

He chuckled. "It's my clan's motto: Those with courage never fail."

He looked at the large painting above the fireplace by the dining room table. It featured two men in the painting, both in their early twenties. They wore kilts with their uniforms. One of the men was his great-great-great grandfather Duncan, and the other man was his great-great- great uncle Daniel. By a solemn twist of fate,

Daniel, the elder of the two men, had perished on a field in France in 1917, just a year before the First World War ended, leaving his younger brother Duncan to become the Earl of Blair.

It was impossible not to grow up in this place surrounded by his family's history, but there had always been a deep sorrow attached to Daniel's memory that made Leith avoid thinking about him. Daniel had bravely done his duty and given his life in the fight. As a Scot, Leith understood war, and although he hated it, he knew it was necessary to fight against the evils in the world. He would defend this land, defend the people of Scotland if he had to.

He lifted up his glass of orange juice to the painting in a silent salute to the two long dead brothers. It was time to get to work. If he was serious about approaching Ainsley about a possible job that might keep her here for a few weeks, he needed to have some kind of idea what he could offer her.

AINSLEY STRETCHED AND YAWNED. THE BED WAS COZY and warm, and she buried her face in the pillow. An unfamiliar but enticing sent lingered on the pillowcase. It smelled of rain, old woods and man. She stilled and slowly opened one eye to peek about the room. She was alone. Leith was gone.

Had she really gotten tipsy on whisky last night and

gone to bed with him? Judging by the way her body was sore in some interesting places, the answer was a definite yes. She blushed all over as she remembered how many times they'd made love. He had been sweet one minute, rough and dirty the next. She'd never known what to expect, and each time they'd come together it had been a sensual adventure. It was as though he'd tried to fit a lifetime of lovemaking into one night.

Ainsley had no regrets, but she was a little embarrassed when she noticed the trashcan by the bed was full of condom wrappers. Was that *seven*? She'd have to hide those wrappers from the Fifes, or they'd think she was some kind of wild, sex maniac.

Ainsley buried her face in her hands and giggled, *actually* giggled. Last night was going down in her personal history as one of the best nights of her life. However, a moment later, her elation deflated. Leith had fled her bed at dawn, which meant he hadn't wanted to stay and enjoy waking up with her.

No, don't do that, she warned herself. She didn't know Leith, didn't know his life. Maybe he had work, or he had something to do that prevented him from remaining with her. She couldn't make assumptions, not until she knew him better.

Which wouldn't happen.

She wasn't staying. She was only here to deliver a ring to some old Scottish lord, and then she was leaving. Leith would be one of those encounters that remained shrouded in mystery and romance.

She got out of bed and took a quick shower in the bathroom across the hall from her bedroom. After she dressed, she went downstairs to the main taproom of the inn.

A lovely middle-aged woman with a sunny smile and warm brown eyes was setting out a feast on the bar counter. Biscuits, toast, poached eggs in pretty little blue and white china egg cups, and a host of other breakfast items enticed her, their aroma delicious. A bowl of something that looked like oatmeal and pitchers of orange juice and ice water were also set out.

"Morning, love," the woman greeted her. "Ye must be Ms. Hazelwood. I'm Molly Fife. I'm glad to hear ye found us last night."

"Oh!" She grinned and held out a hand to the woman. "Call me Ainsley. Your stew was so wonderful last night, just what I needed."

"I imagine it was. My Paul said ye were stranded on the road, and Leith gave ye a ride." She gestured for Ainsley to sit down and set a plate in front of her.

Ainsley's face heated a little. "Yes, Leith was very nice."

"Aye, he is. The delightful rascal," Molly said fondly. "He woke early to bring yer car back for you."

Ainsley halted her spoon just above her plate. "He what?"

Molly chuckled. "The laddie came down here and asked Paul if he would drive out to fetch yer car with him. Leith drove yer car and my husband drove Leith's back. Yer car is waiting for ye outside." Molly set the rental car keys on the counter by Ainsley's plate of food.

Leith had fetched her car for her? That was just as romantic as him staying in bed with her. So many men didn't think about doing little things like that for women. But it made a difference.

"Please tell Paul thank you. Did Leith leave a message from me or anything?" She trailed off at Molly's confused look.

"No, lass, he didna leave a note."

"Oh." Ainsley glumly finished filling her plate. Her low spirits were buoyed somewhat by Molly, who talked to her about the things she must do while she was here in Scotland.

"Ye must go to the castle in Edinburgh and the Isle of Skye. And ye can visit the Kilmartin House, which is only a few miles from here. 'Tis a right lovely museum if you have any interest in history," Molly said. She strapped a large, lovely dark purple apron with painted-on colorful wildflowers around her waist before she cleaned dishes and put fresh glasses in the cabinets.

"Actually, I have a question related to history. I am hoping to find Blair Hall. I was told it was a castle nearby. I'm looking to speak to the Earl of Blair. You wouldn't know who he is, do you?"

At this Molly turned to face her, her eyes full of surprise.

"Lord Blair? Do I know who he is? Of course I do." She gave Ainsley an odd look. "And so do you, lassie. Paul said he shared a room with ye last night."

Ainsley dropped her fork, making a sharp clatter on the plate. "You ... you mean Leith..."

"Aye. *Leith* is Lord Blair. I thought ye kenned who he was."

Ainsley shook her head slowly. "No, he never

mentioned it." She had slept with a Scottish earl? The very man she'd been sent to find? What would Gran think of that?

"Oh well, that's our Leith. He doesna show off his title, especially not to the lassies. He's the humble sort."

And the sexy sort... The kind who had given her a wild, wonderful night. One she would cherish for the rest of her life. Why hadn't she googled him or done more research on the Earl of Blair?

Because Gran had died and Ainsley had been buried in her own grief. Other than buying a plane ticket and booking her room at the inn and a rental car, she hadn't been able to think about the whole mission of bringing the ring back to Scotland.

"What do ye need to speak to Leith about?" Molly asked.

As closed off as Ainsley had felt last night about discussing the ring, she felt safe with Molly Fife. It was as if she'd known the woman for years.

"It's sort of a strange story," she began. "My grandmother died, and she left instructions in her will to return an antique ring to the family of Lord Blair. It was given to my great-great-great-grandmother as a wedding ring. She and the Lord Blair of her day never married, though, because he died in the war."

Molly's lips parted in a gasp. "Ye must mean Daniel! He's the one who perished, bless his soul. He was the young Earl of Blair but when he was killed, his little brother Duncan took the title. Duncan is Leith's ancestor." Molly's eyes filled with a curious light. "'Tis fate, isn't it? Ye and Leith met, and neither of ye kenned yer ancestors were once tied together."

A whisper of a chill rippled over Ainsley's skin, and Molly shuddered. "It's as though someone just walked over my grave," the innkeeper whispered.

Ainsley thought of her grandmother's words about putting ghosts to rest. Perhaps she was correct. Bringing the ring back here was the right thing to do.

Molly cleared her throat, gave a little shake of her head and wiped her hands on her apron.

"Finish yer breakfast. I'll write down some directions for you to reach the castle. It's right on the shore of Loch Awe."

Ainsley ate, but her belly quivered with nerves. She would see Leith again, and she would have to give him the ring. And then what? Go home to an empty apartment? Return to an empty life? Pushing away the instant wave of melancholy and dread at the thought, she accepted Molly's hand-drawn map and directions. They were very well done, with landmarks sketched into the map. Ainsley thanked the woman profusely. She had a terrible sense of direction, and being in a foreign country didn't help.

She checked her purse to make sure the ring and Gran's letter were still inside. Then, she climbed into the rental car. She drove east, following Molly's map as she wound her way down a few paved roads before she turned toward Loch Awe. The skies were clear of clouds. No wind trespassed over the landscape as the she stopped the vehicle facing the loch. The loch lay utterly still, letting the mountain of Ben Cruachan and the ruins of a castle right in front of the mountain reflect back in the water almost like a perfect mirror image. Her breath caught in her throat as she stared at the haunting beauty of the medieval structure.

Something inside her went as still as the waters of the loch. This was the land of her great-great-great-grandmother. She'd been born in these rolling green hills. In fact, she probably sat on the shores of this loch as she gave her heart to a young man who dwelt in that castle. What had she felt when he'd failed to come home? Ainsley couldn't imagine the heartache, the soul-shattering pain of losing the man she loved. Gran had said that the poor woman's grief had driven her across the seas where she'd waited a full decade before marrying someone else. First loves ... especially lost ones ... had a hold on a person's heart, though. Ainsley imagined her ancestor would've lain awake at night, wondering what if ... what if Daniel had come home?

A desperate, bittersweet ache for a long-dead woman and the man she had loved and lost made tears burn in Ainsley's eyes, and she covered her mouth to choke down a sudden sob. In an instant, she understood what Gran had truly wanted her to do. It wasn't just about returning the ring to a family. In some small way, she was bringing her ancestor and Daniel back together after all this time.

She wiped her tears and started driving toward the castle. As she came around the loch and approached the castle, she was stunned to see that while the side facing the loch was in ruins, the rest of the structure had been completely rebuilt from whatever had caused the ruins to the other side. A lovely gravel driveway lined the front of the castle, and another led to a carriage house attached to the south side. When she saw Leith's Land Rover in the open doorway of the carriage house, her heartbeat kicked up a beat with fresh excitement and nerves.

She parked in the front drive rather than in the carriage house. She was a visitor, after all, and she wasn't sure what the protocol was for visiting an earl. Climbing out of the car, she stared up at the massive, impressive structure. Her dark brown ankle boots scraped lightly on the gravel as she walked up to the large oak door. Brass studs jutted out of the wood in a checkered pattern that looked medieval. She touched the stag's head knocker thoughtfully, then lifted it up and brought it down on the door a few times, hoping someone would hear.

Ainsley waited a few minutes, and just when she feared that no one would come to the door, it opened. She came face-to-face with Leith, his eyes widening in shock as he took in the sight of her.

"Ainsley? Are ye all right?" He looked ruggedly attractive this morning in jeans and a white fisherman sweater that clung to his muscled frame. His gaze searched hers, and she was touched by his concern.

"Um … *hi.*" She was tongue-tied as she tried to remember why she was here. Memories of last night flooded her with heat. "This is going to sound crazy, but I have something that belongs to you."

CHAPTER 4

"I have something that belongs to you." Ainsley cleared her throat as she stared at the handsome Scot.

Leith's brows rose. "Something for me?"

She nodded, her throat suddenly thick with emotion. "May I come in?" Returning the ring would require a larger explanation, and she owed it to him to give him the whole story.

His cheeks turned ruddy. "Of course, come in." He opened the large oak door and stepped back, letting her enter.

Walking over the threshold was like stepping into another world ... a medieval one. The great entryway had a stone staircase lined with tapestries that depicted knights of old riding into battle. Swords hung crossed above doorways and suits of armor were tucked in corners, their helmets laced with cobwebs. Remnants of history decorated the stone interior, making every inch of the great hall fascinating. She couldn't help but wonder what these stones had seen over the years.

"This way." Leith gently touched her shoulder, pulling her out of her dreamy thoughts. He led her through an arched doorway to a sitting room. The sitting room's plaster walls had been painted a rich light tan color that paired well with the dark wooden beams spreading across the ceiling. Blue and green plaid carpet, probably the tartan of Leith's family, covered the floor. Gilded, framed portraits of noble but solemn looking ancestors lined the walls. A large, overstuffed dark blue velvet couch and a pair of matching armchairs faced the white and gray marble fireplace at the far end of the room.

"Have a seat, lass. I'll fetch some tea." Leith vanished down the hallway they'd come through, leaving her to marvel at the room. She lingered at a table covered in an old red brocade tablecloth which was faded by sunlight. Old books covered the surface, and she picked one up. Her breath caught as she realized it was a first edition of *Treasure Island*.

Flipping through the pages, she inhaled the musty scent of the timeless adventure story, and it soothed her. Books always created a safe place for her. She reverently set it down and walked up to the nearest portrait. A young man with blond hair and green eyes gazed unseeing past her at some distant past she could only imagine. He was handsome, with a solemn face that held the look of great heartache. She reached up, touching the man's mouth, and a little shiver ran through her.

"It was my great-great-great-uncle, Daniel

Creighton." Leith's voice came from behind her. She turned to see him holding a cup of tea out to her.

"Thank you." She accepted the cup and took a sip. Chamomile and lavender, her *favorite*. Leith was a wonder. He even seemed to know what kind of tea she would like. She turned back to the portrait as Leith moved to stand beside her.

"He died in the First World War," Leith said, his voice soft and full of an old pain that came with having a family that held great legacies full of stories.

"I know," she replied and forced her gaze away from Daniel's portrait to look at Leith.

"Ye know?" Leith asked in surprise.

"Yes. He is why I'm here." She walked toward the couch and sat down. Leith joined her, sitting close by. She set her purse on her lap and dug through it to find the little velvet box, and then she held it out to him.

His face flashed with confusion as he took it. "What's this?"

"It's yours... Or rather, it was his." She nodded over her shoulder at Daniel's portrait.

Leith opened the box, and his gaze sharpened on the ring nestled inside. It was a lovely diamond with a thick gold band.

"No... No... it canna be. This was lost. It..." His throat worked as his eyes lifted to hers in questioning wonder. "Where did ye get this, lass?"

"My grandmother," she replied. Pulling out the letter her grandmother wrote, she gave it to him. "It's why I'm here. She wanted me to bring the ring home. Daniel gave it to my great-great-great-grandmother, Davina."

Leith set the ring box down on the coffee table and took her grandmother's letter when she offered it to him. He read it silently. When he was done, he folded it and gave it back to her.

"We never knew what happened to Davina. She's been one of our family's longest mysteries. After Daniel died, his mother told Davina of Daniel's passing and as the story goes, it broke her heart. Following the chaos of the war, no one knew what became of her after she left Greystone."

"I can fill in the rest of the story," Ainsley replied. "Davina came to New York, and after ten years she married and had children. It wasn't a love match, according to my grandmother, but they were friends and their marriage was built on friendship and respect. Her ring was passed down through the females in my family until it finally came to my grandmother. Davina entrusted it to them, knowing that someday one of us would return it. I am the last woman in my family, so here I am bringing it home."

Strangely, Ainsley felt like crying but she couldn't say why. Bringing the ring home felt good, yet her heart was bleeding at the same time. Seeing Daniel's portrait had unlocked something in her chest that wouldn't stop hurting.

"Daniel and Davina were said to have a once-in-a-lifetime love." Leith removed the ring from the box.

The firelight from the marble fireplace made the diamond at the heart of the ring flash and glint. He studied the gold band, which was abnormally thick. He gently started to pry the ring and its band apart.

"Oh, no, stop! You'll break it—" She reached for the ring, but before she could stop him, the band suddenly...

Unfolded?

She gasped as Leith gently unbound the band into a series of tiny, interconnected gold circles.

"My mother told me about this," he said with a wry smile. "It was made in the 1840s for one of my ancestors when he proposed to the woman he loved. It can be turned into a bracelet." He took Ainsley's wrist without a word and clicked the bracelet around her. The ring's jewels rested in the center of the band on her wrist, just below the back of her hand.

"See?" He stroked her skin by the bracelet. "It's beautiful, isn't it?"

Ainsley's throat tightened with another rush of emotion. "Yes," she breathed; she was watching Leith's face as she said it. He was beautiful too. His gazed had filled with a deep well of love, aroused by thoughts of a long-dead romance between his ancestor and hers. It was impossible not to find that beautiful.

"'Tis one of those things I would try to change if I ever had the ability to slip back in time," he whispered. "I would tell Daniel not to take the hill in that charge. I'd tell him to stay in the trenches with his men. I would've fought the world to bring him back, even if it meant erasing myself from existence."

"You would?" she breathed. She'd never heard anyone talk so deeply of love and wanting to save it.

He lifted up her grandmother's letter again, brushing his thumbs over the words before he met her gaze.

"Aye, I've read his letters to her, the things he said,

the way he *loved* her and how she loved him. They had such a love that I would gladly sacrifice my life in order to give them a happy life together. A love like that is worth fighting for." Leith's eyes burned with a fiery intensity that thrilled and frightened her.

"I've never known a love like that," she confessed.

"Never?" Leith reached up and brushed a lock of her hair behind her ear, his lips parting as he gazed at her mouth. There was a hunger in his fixation on her lips, but also a tenderness that drew her in like she was bewitched.

"Never." She leaned in before she could stop herself, desperate to kiss him again. He curled his fingers around her neck, pulling her toward him in the same instant. Ainsley let the Highland magic of the moment sweep her away.

LEITH FELT CERTAIN HE WAS IN A DREAM. AINSLEY'S lips touched his in an explosion of sweet fire. When he opened the door to find her standing there, he'd been too excited to see her again to ever guess what would bring her to his door. Now here she was, holding a key to his family's past... And all he could think was how much he needed to kiss her, show her what it felt like to experience a love that would be worth fighting the world over to protect.

He kissed her deeply, his tongue gently playing with

hers as he pulled her closer, needing to feel her beside him.

They were strangers with only a shared night of wild passion between them, but perhaps this was the beginning of something more. Something incredible. He wanted it to be. Ainsley leaned back on the couch, lying flat and he followed her, fitting into the crook of her thighs as he continued to kiss her. He wanted to memorize the shape and feel of her mouth so he would never forget it for the rest of his life. Ainsley called to him like no other woman ever had before. Perhaps it was because their ancestors had been so deeply linked, but Leith wanted to know this woman, to learn everything about her and see if this connection could lead to something deeper, something richer.

Ainsley made soft, sweet sighs as he trailed kisses along her jaw to her throat, and her hands dug into his hair, tugging on the strands. Kissing her was like falling through time and space, endlessly spinning in an exquisite kaleidoscope of light and heat.

"What are we doing, Leith?" she whispered as he kissed the shell of her ear. Her skin tasted sweet.

"We're getting lost in each other, lass," he replied as he nibbled on her earlobe. She moaned his name in a blissful way that sent delicious shivers through him.

He kissed her for a long while after that, until the fire began to die and the light slanted in the windows as the sun crept toward the horizon. Only then did he remember where he was and what he was doing. He lifted his head and gazed down at Ainsley's face.

"Stay with me," he said suddenly, surprising even himself at the sudden request.

Ainsley's eyes widened. "Stay?" She formed the word slowly, her face still soft with the glow of his kisses.

"Yes, stay. Ye want a job? I might have one for ye. Blair Castle needs a public relations specialist, and I can pay. Just … *stay*." He felt deep in his bones that the ring had brought him Ainsley for a reason. Like many people in Scotland, he believed in fate and in tales of love and magic. She had been brought here for a reason; he was certain of it.

"Where would I stay?" she asked as he lifted her up to sit in the circle of his arms.

"Here. We have plenty of rooms. Stay in one of yer choosing."

She bit her bottom lip. "That would be crazy … to stay here. I mean, my life—"

"Last night, ye said ye had no one to go back to. Maybe ye are meant to go forward. Give me a month, see if ye wish to help."

"A month." She studied his face and looked around the room with a sheepishly adorable smile. "It would be an adventure, wouldn't it?"

"Yes, it would," he agreed. "Come on. Let me show ye the castle and grounds. Then we can run into town and fetch yer luggage from Paul's place."

He rose from the couch and took her hand, wanting to show her his world.

BLAIR HALL WAS BREATHTAKING. AINSLEY FOLLOWED Leith from room to room, that strange sense of connection to him and this place growing stronger. She was introduced to a few men and women who helped clean and care for the castle. The housekeeper and cook, Mrs. Tibbons, had eyed her critically until she heard about the story of the family ring's return. Then the cook was cupping her cheeks and kissing her forehead as if she had known Ainsley all her life.

"My great-great grandmother was a dear friend to Davina. Everyone always wanted to know what happened to her. She left it all behind when Daniel didn't return, and we had no way of knowing where she went."

It amazed Ainsley to learn how much her ancestor and the love story about the tragic Earl of Blair had meant to this little piece of Scotland. She'd told Mrs. Tibbons what Davina's life had been like after reaching New York. The woman was delighted, and she wiped a few tears from her eyes.

"Ye did a good thing, lassie, bringing the ring home," Mrs. Tibbons said, her eyes bright with tears. "I think I'll make some Cranachan for ye both tonight. Now, off with ye! I need my space in the kitchens to work my magic."

Leith put an arm around Ainsley's waist and they left the kitchen.

"What is ... Cranachan?" she asked in a whisper.

"It's a traditional Scottish pudding, a bit like a trifle. There are layers consisting of whipped cream, toasted oats, and juicy raspberries... Oh and a touch of whisky." He winked at her.

"Is there whisky in everything in this country?" she asked.

"Most everything," he teased. "It wouldna be Scottish if it didna have at least a bit of whisky."

Leith retrieved her coat from the sitting room and grabbed his own from an ancient-looking coat closet that had a mound of Wellington rubber boots below the coats.

"Put on a pair of these." He nodded at the Wellingtons. "Leave yer shoes here. I want to show ye the grounds."

"So, what exactly is the job that you mentioned?" Ainsley asked as she removed her boots and donned a pair of Wellingtons. She followed Leith out the oak front door. They left the castle and began to traverse the gravel path that ran in front of the castle and headed toward the loch.

"When we dined at the inn last night, I mentioned that I kenned someone who would hire ye for publicity. If ye havena guessed, it's me, lass. This place could use a bit of help. That show that all you lassies fancy, I forget what it's called..."

"*Highlander, My Love?*" Ainsley asked, grinning.

"That one." Leith chuckled when he looked at her.

"It has put Scotland back in the mind of tourists. They love the castles, the lochs, the history. I want Blair to be a part of that. Only I dinna ken how to bring people here."

Ainsley and Leith stopped to admire Loch Awe and the way the brilliant blue skies were now clear of last night's storm. The air smelled clean, full of a dozen scents that filled her head with romantic images of Scotland: rain, trees, soil, farmland and old stones. They all carried aromas that, when combined, was like breathing in magic. They gave her a sudden flood of ideas of how to get people to discover Blair Castle.

"Would you consider opening up your castle for visitors?"

Leith faced her, a thoughtful expression on his face. "Visitors? Ye mean like a museum?"

"Maybe. You could partner with the Kilmartin House museum. Molly told me about it. Kilmartin House could offer day trips out to Blair Castle to just tour the grounds and some of the rooms. You could also open your castle to actual guests. Weddings and charity events would be wildly popular. Or you could even just host regular hotel guests. My friend from college got married in Scotland and stayed at a Victorian era hunting lodge in southern Scotland. I wish I'd been able to go to her wedding, but I couldn't get the time off. My friend said the place where she stayed was basically like a small hotel but the family who owned it had their private quarters that were open to guests."

Leith turned to study the castle, his gaze drifting over his home with a new appreciation.

"We need to rebuild the damaged part of the structure. I canna imagine it would be safe to have guests around until I've done so."

Ainsley followed his gaze. "What happened to it?" The damage to the part of the castle facing the loch was clearly old, but she wasn't sure how old.

"There was a lightning strike in 1827 and a fire started, burning down part of the castle. No one was harmed and the residents at the time managed to save several paintings and tapestries before the ceiling collapsed over that picture gallery where the fire occurred. The rain thankfully put out the blaze before it could spread."

Images of a fire filled Ainsley's head, and her heart ached for the past. She was glad that no one had been hurt and that the castle was still standing. It would be a terrible loss to have something so beautiful destroyed.

They continued to tour the gardens and finally reached the paddocks near the loch where a herd of Highland cows were feeding on grass. A man dressed in outdoor work clothes stood by the fence, keeping an eye on the cattle. He wore a traditional tam-o'-shanter, a hat which looked like a French beret but had a small puffed ball on it rather than a thin felt point in the center.

Leith called out to the man. "Dougal!"

The man turned in their direction, scratching lightly at his salt-and-pepper beard.

"Laird," he greeted. Then he saw Ainsley. "Is this the lassie you rescued?" The man's gaze turned impish.

Leith's face turned red as he shot Ainsley a glance.

"Did you tell *everyone* about my disaster last night?"

she asked, not sure whether to be embarrassed or amused.

"The laddie talked about you for a full hour after breakfast this morning," Dougal informed her with a sly wink.

"I didna do that," Leith argued.

"He did, lass. He fair swooned over ye as he spoke," Dougal whispered loudly, clearly enjoying teasing Leith.

As they talked, one of the large brown, hairy cows wandered over to the fence. Ainsley reached a hand over and petted the cow's snout while it stared at her with soulful brown eyes. She loved how when Leith spoke about them, it sounded like he was saying "hairy coos."

"People would love these cows. I would add them into the marketing materials," she said to Leith.

"Marketing materials?" Dougal echoed. "What's the lass talking about?"

"Ms. Hazelwood may be staying here for a few weeks, and is considering how to improve the castle's income by attracting tourists."

The older man harrumphed. "Then you'd better not forget to warn the tourists about the midges, lass. No one will want to be in this pasture in the summer."

"Midges?" Ainsley asked.

"Aye, blasted little biters," Dougal muttered.

"Are they some sort of mosquito or more like chiggers?" Ainsley asked Leith. She hated chiggers. She'd been bitten by several one summer when she was young, and it had been awful.

"They are a bit like mosquitoes. Only the females bite, and it stings something fierce. Being on the west side of Scotland, we have the worst midges. We suffer from May to October every year. They gather on most of the grass areas and near the cows."

"Hmm... So your castle gift shop will need to sell strong insect repellent."

"And midge hats," Dougal added as he braced a foot on the railing of the fence and studied her with amusement.

"Dare I ask what a midge hat is?" Ainsley glanced between the two men.

"'Tis a wide brimmed hat with a net that secures around yer neck," Leith supplied. "Dougal, you're scaring her. Midges are not so bad if ye prepare yerself." Leith grabbed Ainsley by the waist and guided her away from Dougal, who laughed heartily as they walked away.

"He seems colorful," Ainsley said with a grin.

"He is. He'll be the most Scottish man ye'll ever meet while ye stay here."

"What's his position at the castle?"

"Officially Dougal is the groundskeeper, but he handles a lot more. I grew up with him and after my father passed, he became a bit like an uncle to me."

"He would make a fantastic tour guide."

Leith laughed and the hearty sound echoed off the mountain behind the castle. "Don't tell him that, lass. He doesna need a bigger ego than he already has."

Ainsley stopped halfway back to the castle as she watched distant clouds roll down the Argyll mountains toward the castle. She grasped Leith's hand, halting him as something came over her. It felt like she was standing in two centuries at the same time. Davina had been long dead by generations before Ainsley had been born, but she swore her ancestor felt alive to her. In that moment, she knew she would stay here for a month to help Leith. She wanted to do it for Davina and for herself.

"I'll do it. I'll help you," she told him. Their gazes locked and that sense of rightness, of a golden purpose, filled her so strongly that she felt like she was glowing on the inside with the realization that this was what she'd been meant to do her entire life.

"Ye mean it?" Leith asked.

She nodded. She couldn't explain that she felt like she belonged here with him in this beautiful place. It would sound too crazy, but it was the truth.

"Show me everything," she asked.

Leith pulled her closer until their bodies touched front to front. He held her to him, one arm wrapped gently but possessively around her lower back. His hand curved around her cheek as he lowered his head to hers, and then kissed her softly, sweetly, his lips *burning* in the best way. They shouldn't be this close, shouldn't be kissing, if he was to become a client. But right then, she couldn't bring herself to care about the ethics of her possible job. All she cared about was tasting this man's kiss and breathing in the clean air of her ancestors.

"All right ... sassenach," he breathed.

"What's a sassenach?" she asked. She thought she might have heard it once or twice on the show *Highlander, My Love*, but she'd never known what it meant.

His chuckle warmed her straight down to her toes. "Ye have a lot to learn, lassie."

CHAPTER 5

"I thought ye'd would want to see these." Leith joined her at the dining room table, which had become Ainsley's command center over the last week since she'd moved into Blair Castle. The surface of the fancy table was covered with stacks—guidebooks for Scotland, museum pamphlets, and other papers that she had collected or printed to create a publicity plan for the castle. This project for his estate had been a welcome distraction to keep her safely away from Leith's bed.

Ainsley lifted her gaze from her laptop to see what Leith held out, but her focus was drawn immediately to his face and the striking beauty of his masculine features. Would she ever not react like this to him? She forced herself to pull her gaze toward what he held in his hand—a stack of letters bound with a faded red ribbon. She took the letters, her fingers moving over the aged paper. A name written out in scrawling script on the top letter grabbed her attention.

Davina.

"Are these what I think they are?" she asked as Leith took a seat at the table beside her.

"Aye, it took me a while to find them in the family papers." His eyes softened as he watched her examine the letters.

"How do you still have these?"

"Before Daniel departed for the front, he left most of his letters from Davina in his parents' keeping. I heard that when Davina left, she kept the engagement ring but presented the letters that she received from Daniel to his parents so that their letters would remain together. Their entire love story is here in these pages, including the last letter, which was retrieved from Daniel's body and brought home by a fellow solider." Leith helped her turn the letters over. The bottom one was marred with rust-colored droplets that she realized too late must be blood. *Daniel's blood.* Her chest constricted as she pulled the last letter out and then with tender care removed it from the envelope.

My dearest darling,

This is what the other fellows here call the blood letter, the one we hope you ladies never have to receive. If you're reading these words now, it means I failed you. I never made it home, and we never got married in that little chapel in Greystone.

I've done my best not to think of death. Someone here said that it must surely be an adventure, but for me, I hope it will be quiet. The sound of guns, the scream of horses, and the moans of dying men filled my ears these last few months. The dark and the silence would be a relief. But in that place of rest and endless night I will dream of what should have been, had the darkness in men's hearts not prevailed three years ago. How grand and noble it would have been to hide away with you in-between the loch and the hills, basking in that place of grandeur which bears the name of our home.

No one speaks here of the longing for home. It cuts a man's heart too deeply to speak of bright and pretty memories, to think of lands which had never seen a trench, or the fog of toxic gas. I will dream of stepping into the library at Blair Castle and finding you waiting for me, your face shining in the Scottish sunlight and your eyes alight with the magic of the land we both love.

I will dream of love's highest gift, that in loving you I loved my dearest friend and shared a passion that will burn until the light of the last star fails to shine. Promise me, if you find your-self reading this one day, that you will still seek joy in the world, that you will not fall into this quiet night with me, not until you are an old woman surrounded by great-grandchildren. Only then should you slip away and join me.

Yours in every dream,

Daniel

Ainsley wasn't aware that she was crying until the words on the page blurred and her nose stung. She set the paper down on the table and wiped furiously at her tears.

"I'm sorry, lass." Leith pulled her out of her chair and settled her onto his lap before he wrapped his arms around her. "I kenned it would make ye weep, but ye needed to read it. Ye needed to know what ye did was right."

"What I did?" Ainsley lifted her face up to stare at him.

"Coming here to an unknown land and giving something precious from yer family to someone ye didn't even ken."

"But the ring belongs here. I couldn't keep it, knowing what it means to your family." She glanced down at her wrist, but it was bare. She had removed the ring bracelet after Leith had put it on her, and she had insisted he put it in the jewelry vault in his study where it would be safe.

"Perhaps it does belong here, and I think ye belong here too, lass," Leith murmured before he pressed his lips in the crown of her hair.

Sometimes she couldn't believe that it had only been a week since she had moved into Blair Castle for her month-long work on the revitalization project. A week since she had let herself get carried away by this man and his touch.

That first day, she'd told him that if she worked for him, they couldn't sleep together. It simply wasn't professional. Leith had flashed her a soft grin as if amused at her declaration rather than upset by it. Yet he had respected her request. He'd let her have her space and hadn't come to her bedchamber even once in the past week. It wasn't an easy thing to admit that she felt disappointed by that, but she was glad he had respected her wishes.

She shuddered as another wave of emotions, still so raw from reading the letters, made her shake in his arms.

"Shh," he whispered soothingly as he rested his lips against her brow. This time when she shivered, it was because his touch still deeply affected her. It was as though some part of her had been trapped in ancient slumber—yet now it had awakened. It still amazed her that she felt such a pull to him, even before she learned who he was. Perhaps Molly's belief that fate had brought them together was true. After all, their ancestors had once been so tightly bound. It was as though patterns of love ran through the fabric of generations.

"Ye should read the rest of the letters later. Ye have plenty of time." He gave her waist a gentle squeeze. "Now, open yer eyes and let me see ye smile."

She managed a watery smile.

"I have surprise for ye," he said, offering a boyish grin, which faintly crinkled the corners of his eyes. Seeing his delight made her chest expand with a quiet joy she couldn't quite explain.

"Surprise? It had better be something other than heartbreaking letters."

He chuckled, the rich timber of the sound warming her all over. She loved the sound of his laugh, even those rough chuckles. "No, no more letters. I want to take ye to the local Highland games, which will be starting at nine."

She checked her watch. It was only eight in the morning. She'd gotten an early start each day since she slept really well in the castle's quiet peace.

"Highland games? What are those?"

"Sassenach," he laughed softly. "I forgot ye ken very little of our traditions. The Highland games are traditional festivals of local sports and culture."

"Oh, kind of like an American country fair?"

"Aye, a bit like that. Can ye be ready to leave in a few minutes?"

She nodded. "Yes, just let me grab a coat." Ainsley slid off his lap and darted up to her chambers to grab her coat and a small purse.

Leith waited for her at the foot of the main stairs. They took his SUV since it handled the differing road conditions in this part of Scotland. She'd been relieved to return her rental car since Leith could take her anywhere she needed to go while she stayed here.

"How often do they hold the Highland games?" Ainsley asked as they drove through the beautiful countryside.

"About once a year. They occur all over Scotland, usually between mid-June and late August. Ours is late in September."

Ainsley was eager to see what Leith was so clearly excited about.

"I haven't been to the games in a few years."

When they reached the games arena, Ainsley found herself staring at a vast field which was designed to look like a track-and-field competition, including an oval track around the field. Surrounding the entire oval area were a mix of stands—skill-testing carnival games, others run by local charities that were raising funds by selling fried sausage sandwiches, baked goods, bottles of beer and *Irn-bru*, which Leith explained was a bright orange-colored Scottish soft drink. After Leith parked his car, they walked toward the crowd that had gathered by the infield and the track.

"Ahh, we're just in time, lass." Leith slipped his hand in hers and pulled her along. He squeezed them through the crowds and put her body in front of his, holding her hips with his hands. In front of them, a group of people were marching and playing cheery music. Leith leaned closer to whisper in her ear.

"That's the pipe band." He nodded at the group of musical players who wore kilts and uniforms. An older gentleman with a white beard carried a bass drum and led the players. "That's the local clan chief Tom MacQuarrie." Ainsley had been fascinated to learn that clans were still legally recognized groups in Scotland, and that chiefs still managed much of the clan activities.

The bagpipe notes trilled in the air as the players made a full circle around the vast area of the games. Ainsley turned her head slightly to watch Leith's face during the little parade. His countenance was full of joy. She envied his love of this place and these people. It was a wonderful thing to belong somewhere and to love it so fiercely. The crowd cheered as the band finished, and then everyone dispersed to the nearby food stands or to watch the athletes as they started their games in the infield.

"Let's grab a Scotch ale and watch the Highland dancers first." Leith took her to a food stand and bought two ales before he escorted her to a raised platform nearby. Several girls who wore either red or blue sweater tops, red or blue plaid shirts, and plaid socks were stretching and readying themselves for the dance competition.

"They look so young," Ainsley mused. Some of the girls had to be in grade school.

"They are. Many girls learn to dance at a young age. See how they pair up? They always dance in pairs or groups of four," Leith observed.

Ainsley saw two girls take their place. They wore soft shoes like ballet slippers but without the hardened toes. A young man with a set of bagpipes began to play a lively tune for them. The two girls danced while Ainsley watched, utterly mesmerized. The girls remained on the balls of their feet for almost the entire dance, keeping perfectly balanced as their feet fluttered toward and away from their bodies in delicate patterns. It was like watching a pair of brightly colored butterflies dancing around each other.

As the dance ended, Ainsley clapped loudly. Then her jaw dropped as the dance coordinator brought two large swords onto the stage. He set them down to create a cross that made four squares.

"What—" she began.

"Just watch, lass." Leith chuckled and gave her waist a gentle squeeze.

Two older dancers stepped out on the platform and took their spots. As music started, Ainsley realized these women were not only talented but well trained as they danced in and out of the crossed swords on the floor. Their toes fluttered and tapping so close to the blades that Ainsley held her breath until they finished.

"That was incredible." She took Leith's hand as they walked toward the large field where an announcer was hyping up the crowd.

"My mother was quite a good dancer, especially with the Highland fling. That was the first dance that you saw."

"That's amazing. Do most girls learn?"

"The ones who like tradition, and the ones who have a talent for dancing. Ye can earn scholarships and money awards for winning competitions."

Leith stopped at the far end of the field, where several bulky men in kilts stood next to a large pile of logs that looked like telephone poles. On one end of each long log, there were three or four inches of black tape wound around the wood.

"My father was talented at this one, the caber toss."

"The caber? You mean the giant logs?"

"Aye."

"Was your father a big man?" she asked.

Leith was muscled, but he was not huge, not like the men standing at the edge of the log pile.

"No, he was lean, like me, but he was strong. He always used to say it's not how big yer muscles are, but how ye use them."

"He sounds like a smart man," Ainsley replied.

Leith's eyes softened as he gazed at the caber tossers. "He was."

"So how does this work?" She nodded at the caber tossing group.

"Watch this fellow." Leith pointed at the first man in line for the caber toss, who was dressed in a dark blue kilt and a green sweater. The man rolled up his sleeves and lifted up one of the cabers until it stood vertical. He crouched down and securely grasped the base of the caber in his hands and used the groove between his neck and shoulder to keep the caber vertical as he stood up. Then he started to walk slowly, before speeding up.

"He'll release it soon by throwing it up high in the air," Leith said.

The competitor started to run full out, using his momentum as he drove forward with his legs and hips. Then he pushed up with his hands to fling the caber, clearly trying to make it flip over in the air.

"If he can fully flip it and point the end that has the black tape in his hands to land in the opposite direction, it's considered good and it's called a twelve o'clock toss. If the tape that is near his hands now fails to flip over, then it's considered a six o'clock toss. It takes strength and skill. So you can see why in the old days, clan chiefs would select their strongest men to battle on the game field, in hopes it would end or prevent any clan feuds and real battles."

THEY WATCHED THE OTHER CABER TOSSERS BEFORE moving on to the other events. There was a weight-throwing event which Ainsley realized was close to shot-put. And she marveled at the "weight over the bar" event where men tossed a fifty-six-pound weight over a high bar.

"No two Highland games are alike. Some are large, and some are small, like ours."

Ainsley and Leith circled the field enjoying the events, and when Ainsley mentioned she was hungry, Leith purchased two fried sausage sandwiches before the events of the day began to wind down. They were sitting at one of the picnic tables, drinking the last of their ales when the town chieftain Tom MacQuarrie walked over to them.

"Lord Blair, do ye mind leaving yer bonnie lass for a wee bit to join my team for the tug-of-war? We're a man short, and ye could show yer lass what a Scottish lord is made of." Tom winked at Ainsley.

"Ye dinna mind a skinny man like me?" Leith asked the chieftain with a charming grin.

"Ye're no skinny, man. Ye're built just like yer father, and he always headed the tug-of-war in his day." Tom lifted a booted foot, placed it on the edge of Leith's bench seat, then rested his forearm on his raised knee while he talked to them. Ainsley did her best not to look in the direction of Tom's raised kilt, lest she find the answer to what a Scotsman wore underneath.

"All right, ye talked me into it, MacQuarrie." Leith gave a mock sigh and winked at Ainsley.

Tom clapped his hands together. "Then our victory is secured. Now, dinna be thinking ye distracted me, laddie... Who is this fine lady?" He held out a hand in greeting to Ainsley.

"This is Ainsley Hazelwood. She's helping me with drawing tourists into Blair Castle."

"Is she now? We could use a bit more tourists here," Tom informed her. "Maybe when ye finish with the laddie, ye can visit me and help me draw people to the town?" he asked hopefully.

"I might be able to." She didn't want to say no to the

chieftain, so she kept her answer vague just in case she wasn't able to pay him a visit.

"Wonderful! And dinna mind me, lass, I just need to steal yer man for a wee bit."

"Oh, he's not—" She didn't have the time to correct Tom by saying that Leith wasn't her man because the chief grasped Leith by the elbow and dragged him to his feet. They walked toward an area where a large thick rope lay on the ground. A line of yellow tape had been placed on the muddy grass to mark the middle, and a red cloth had been knotted around the middle of the rope. Several men were removing their shirts or sweaters. Leith removed his own sweater, and Ainsley quickly rushed forward to take it from him.

"Why are you taking off your clothes? It's *freezing*," Ainsley whispered. She'd worn her coat all day and couldn't imagine how cold it would be to strip down to nothing.

Leith grinned roguishly. "'Tis because of the mud, lass." He nodded at the damp, muddy earth beneath his feet. "We dinna want to ruin all of our clothes, ye ken."

"Oh ... right." She dodged back when she realized her own boots were covered with the thick, dark mud.

"No kiss for luck?" Leith called out to her, that damn smile of his pulling her back to him. He curled an arm around her waist when she got close, and he caught her lips with his in a quick but sinful kiss that made her toes curl. She could taste the beer on his lips and feel the heat of his bare chest pressed to her breasts. When he drew back, he stroked his thumb over her bottom lip, smiling at her in a way that did funny things to her heart. She continued to gaze at him in a daze, momentarily unable to remember why she shouldn't be kissing him.

"Now out of the way, love, or you'll get muddy too," he teased and gave her bottom a little swat. She stumbled backward into the waiting crowd, still clutching his sweater in her arms.

"He yours?" a woman asked Ainsley as she stepped up beside her.

"What?" Ainsley glanced toward the woman, who seemed to be in her late forties. She was pretty and polished, but she exuded an air of command that called attention to her. Her clothes were expensive, her blond hair perfectly styled. Ainsley knew a woman with money when she saw one. And based on her accent, she was a fellow American.

"That tall glass of whisky there," the woman said as she pointed to Leith.

"Oh, well it's..." She didn't know quite how to explain what she and Leith were to each other.

The woman laughed softly. "Complicated, huh? The best ones usually are."

Ainsley smiled sheepishly. "You could say that. It's kind of a crazy story, actually."

"Oh? I'd love to hear it, and it looks like we have some time before they start the event."

The men on the two sides of the tug-of-war were discussing rules with the judge, and Leith was clearly being consulted by the judge and MacQuarrie. Ainsley quickly shared the story of how she had ended up here in Scotland and how their paths had crossed with the return of the antique ring.

The woman listened intently, her brown eyes sharp with intensity. "Now that *is* a story." She reached into her purse. "My name is Sarah Shelton. I'm a producer for the show *Highlander, My Love*." She gave Ainsley her business card.

"*Highlander, My Love*? I'm *obsessed* with that show," Ainsley confessed. "I've watched the first three seasons at least five times."

Sarah's face brightened. "I love hearing that. We're secretly scouting locations right now for season four. I've never been to one of these Highland games before, so I thought I'd drop by while I was in the area."

Ainsley took the woman's business card and retrieved one of her own from her purse.

"I'm Ainsley Hazelwood. This is my personal email. I do PR work. I just recently left my past firm, and I'm working for Blair Castle at the moment. It would make a fantastic location for you. It's not far if you want to come by and see it."

"Really? That would be fantastic," Sarah said. A breeze drew her hair into her eyes, and she brushed her blond locks away from her face.

"Blair Castle sits right on the edge of Loch Awe, only half an hour from here."

"You're kidding? I just drove past it yesterday and wanted to visit, but I had a meeting to go to and couldn't stop. Could I swing by tomorrow?"

"I'll need to check with Leith. He's the owner, but I think he'll be fine with it."

"Great. Tell him we pay well for location shoots these days since the show is doing well. Also, I've just had an idea..." Sara tapped her phone and called someone. "Hey, it's Sarah. Yeah... You want to visit a castle with me tomorrow? I promise it will be worth it... Great. I'll pick you up tomorrow and let you know what time." Then she hung up and met Ainsley's confused gaze. "Sorry, that was the show's head writer. She's here looking for inspiration with me. She's writing a spinoff series for us set in the present day with plot lines that tie to the past. I have a feeling that the story you just told me might be something she'd want to hear."

"My story?" Ainsley gasped.

"Oh yeah," Sarah grinned. "A long-lost ring, a man and a woman who fall in love just like their star-crossed ancestors? That would make one hell of a TV season. When you find out whether we can drop by tomorrow, text me the time." Sarah winked, and then she walked off toward the parking lot.

Ainsley felt like she was floating on a cloud. She turned around at the piercing whistle which indicated the start of the tug-of-war game. The men on both sides strained to win. The tourists and crowds of locals cheered for each side. It seemed like two sides were evenly matched.

"Pull, Leith!" Ainsley screamed, her heart racing as she watched him at the front of his team's rope. They struggled for several long minutes, and she had a chance to admire Leith's muscles, which tightened with the tug he gave. His veins grew visible beneath his skin as he fought the men on the other side of the rope.

He gritted his teeth, and he bellowed at his team.

"Pull, laddies, *pull*!" His roar echoed off the distant mountains.

Leith's team took a collective breath and gave a hard tug at the end of the rope. The men on the other side jerked forward and went flying into the mud face-first. Leith's team—the victors—also tumbled backward, crashing down into the muddy ground on their bottoms. The people cheered as the men who'd held the rope all clapped each other on the shoulders. Leith got to his feet, laughing with Tom. Both men were splattered with mud.

"I swear ye're a lucky charm, laddie," Tom said as he escorted Leith back to where Ainsley stood.

"You won," Ainsley said, feeling giddy as she stared at Leith and his mud-splattered chest.

"Keep looking at me like that, lass, and I'll kiss you and ruin your pretty sweater," he warned with a devious glint in his green eyes.

"I'm tempted to let you," she admitted, her voice breathless.

Leith tilted her chin up and leaned in carefully, so that only their lips met as he kissed her. Her lips opened for his and his tongue swept inside, dancing with hers. For a long moment, she was simply lost in this man and basking in the glow of his kiss. When they finally drew apart, he was smiling at her like she'd just given him the keys to a chest of gold.

"Let's go home, I'm *starving*," he said. But it didn't seem like he was talking about food, based on the way the lust gleamed in his eyes. She was hungry too, for him—and she shouldn't be.

Oh no... She couldn't let herself fall into that trap again and sleep with him, no matter how much she wanted to. If she wanted to be professional, she had to remind him that they couldn't be in a relationship. That meant avoiding the hot Scot and the temptation his kisses offered.

CHAPTER 6

"Ach! Look at the state of ye!" Mrs. Timmons gasped as Leith and Ainsley stepped into the kitchens. Leith held back a laugh as he knew that his appearance was no doubt a shock for his sensible housekeeper. After all, he was half naked and covered with mud.

Leith reached for Mrs. Timmons as if to hug her, and she screeched. "No, not covered in mud like that, ye won't!" She swatted at him with a spatula, keeping him at bay. "Why are ye half naked?" Mrs. Timmons demanded.

"Tug-of-war at the games, Mrs. Timmons," he answered. "I didna want to ruin my sweater." What he didn't tell his housekeeper was that he also liked how having his body partially bare kept Ainsley's desire-filled gaze on him.

Till now, he had done his best to respect Ainsley's "no sex with clients" rule—but he was done with that.

She belonged here, she belonged with him, and he intended to show her what that meant. *Tonight.*

"Ye had better wash off that mud, or the maids will have yer head for tracking it through the house." Mrs. Timmons resumed kneading dough for bread, her apron stained lightly with splotches of flour as she worked.

"Come on, lass." Leith took Ainsley's hand in his. She still clutched his sweater in her other hand. Her eyes swept over his skin again, a blush staining her cheeks.

"Dinner will be ready in two hours! Dinna be late, or it will be cold," Mrs. Timmons hollered at their backs as they left the kitchen.

"Leith—" Ainsley began when he tugged her into his bedchamber.

"Hush, lass," he murmured as he closed the door behind them. "Ye said yer piece about us not being together. I was patient for a week, but now 'tis my turn."

Ainsley's eyes widened adorably with shock as he toed off his boots and reached for the buttons of his jeans.

"I thought you said we were going to talk?" she sputtered as he unzipped his pants.

"I didna say I was going to speak. I said it was *my turn.*" He moved toward her, capturing her waist and lifting her up as he carried her to the adjoining bathroom. She gasped as he set her down and briefly let go of her just long enough to turn the shower on. Then he stripped off her clothes. She muttered halfhearted protests until she was down her to panties and underwear.

"Leith, seriously, this isn't professional—"

"Ye're bloody right this isna professional. But yer mine, and I've been patient with ye lass. Now I mean to show ye that we belong to each other, no matter what our business relationship is."

He bent and tugged her panties down her legs, then he unclasped her bra in a swift move. She squealed with shock. Gently, he urged her into the shower stall ahead of him.

"Are we going to talk about this?" she demanded. But all he did was admire the way the hot water poured over her skin, creating ribbons of clear rivers over her breasts and hips.

Leith removed his jeans and socks before he stepped into the stall with her. Then he sealed them both inside, letting the steam warm their chilled bodies. Mud that had dried and caked on his skin softened and washed away. He hastily scrubbed bodywash over himself to make sure he was clean before he turned to her. She was watching him with half-lidded eyes as he ran his hands over his body.

"Like what ye see, lass?" he asked in a silken whisper.

"You know I do," she replied, her face reddening again.

Holding out a hand to her, Leith let out a sigh of relief as she placed her fingers in his. Ainsley's gaze lifted from his body to his face. Stark vulnerability showed in her brown eyes as he pulled her into his arms. He wanted to hold her, feel her heartbeat against his and offer her the comfort of his body.

When they were skin to skin, he tilted her face up for a kiss. His heartbeat throbbed in his ears as he covered her mouth with his. Ainsley's soft lips opened beneath his own, and he savored her sweet taste. He had to convince her that this thing between them was more than just sex. It ran deeper than the sea. It felt as solid and real as the earth beneath his feet. He'd never felt so sure of anything in his life as the way he felt sure about her. Their connection was not something to run from, but to embrace. Yet he knew that Ainsley worried about the unknown.

"Tell me your fears," he whispered in her ear.

"My fears?" she echoed, her hand settling on his shoulders. Her nails dug in slightly as she moved closer to him. He didn't mind.

"You're afraid of this. Tell me why." He kissed her again, long and lingering, determined to remind her how beautiful this thing between them was. He nibbled on her lips, drawing a sigh from her. She pulled even closer to him as she kissed him back. A long moment later, she seemed to remember he'd asked her a question.

"We live an ocean apart," she said. "That's a big thing, to start." Her lashes fluttered as she stared at his lips and then leaned in again to kiss him. The soft, sweet touch of her lips was heaven itself. He slid a hand down her back to gently cup her bottom as he deepened the kiss for a long moment.

Then he pulled back again. "So move in with me. Leave that life behind and return to the land of yer ancestors like Davina."

Her doe-brown eyes softened when he mentioned Davina's name.

Her gaze dropped to the floor. "I'm afraid you think

we should live out some fantasy simply because our ancestors were in love."

"I'm not Daniel, and I ken ye're not Davina. But I believe in fate, Ainsley. I believe that while the destiny of our ancestors was star-crossed, I feel perhaps they were leading us toward each other."

"You can't know that," she argued.

"No one kens their fate with certainty, but my heart feels it all the same." He took one of her hands and placed her palm over his chest above his heart and held it there with his own.

He stroked his thumb over her bottom lip. "What does yer heart tell ye about us?"

She licked her lips. "It makes me want to do something stupid, something foolish that might hurt me."

"Like falling in love?" he asked.

She nodded and glanced away. He gently guided her face back to his.

"Ye need never hide from me, lass. *Never.*"

"Then..." She hesitated. "You think you might love me someday?"

He couldn't stop the sudden grin that spread across his face. "Lass, I loved ye the moment ye rolled down yer window that rainy night and looked at me. I loved ye then, and I have loved ye every moment since then. I will love ye until we're dust and bones." Yes, they'd only met seven days ago. Yes, that time was short. But his heart knew what his heart wanted.

"Leap with me into the unknown, Ainsley," he urged. "Be brave with me, lass."

Her gaze searched his for a long moment before she stood up on her tiptoes and kissed him, hard and desperate. Her longing was so palpable that his heart answered immediately. He moved her back to pin her against the shower wall and then lifted her up to impale her on his shaft. They shared a groan at the connection as he sank fully inside her. She wound her arms around his, kissing him as they rocked rhythmically together. Every time he sank his cock into her wet heat, he never wanted to leave.

"Oh God..." Ainsley murmured and wrapped her legs around his waist.

"That's it, love, take me deep," he encouraged in a gruff whisper as she rocked on him. The hot water poured over his back, streaming down between their bodies as they made love. She tightened her thighs around his hips as she came apart, and he bathed in the beauty of her expression of bliss. Then he carried her to the marble seat at the back of the shower and sat down with her on his lap. He gripped her ass and guided her to ride him harder, moving her faster and faster until he came deep inside her. They both stilled a moment later, clinging to one another.

"I forgot a condom," he breathed. God, how could he become so distracted by her that he overlooked something so important?

"It's okay. I'm on the pill, Leith." She stroked the fingers soothingly over the back of his neck.

"For the record, I adore children," he said. "When ye're ready." His words made her blush adorably.

"Me too, but I'm not ready for one yet," she replied. Then she kissed him again and he found himself lost in her taste. He fisted his hand in her wet hair, lightly curling his fingers in the silky strands. He was still inside her, still connected to her in the most intimate way, and the pleasure of kissing her was beyond imagining. Her inner muscles clenched around him as he thrust his tongue in and out of her lips, playfully mimicking their lovemaking.

"Christ, lass, that feels like heaven," he breathed as he feathered his lips over her neck.

"We should probably get out of here before Mrs. Timmons thinks we've drowned." Ainsley nibbled on his earlobe and giggled.

"Good point," he agreed. "I better wash ye, since I've made ye quite *dirty*," he teased.

He stood and eased out of her body before he set her down on her feet. They washed each other slowly, simply savoring the intimate right to touch each other. When at last they exited the shower, he wrapped her in a large, fluffy bath towel before he wrapped a second one around his hips.

"Oh my God!" Ainsley exclaimed as she whirled to face him. "I just remembered! I need to text Sarah." She ran into the bedroom wearing only her towel.

"Who's Sarah?" he asked as he followed her into the room. She was still clutching her towel around her body with one hand while digging through her small purse on the floor with the other.

"Sarah Shelton... I met her at the games today while

you were in the tug-of-war competition." She whooped in triumph as she found her cell phone and also pulled out a business card.

"I'm still lost, lass. Who is Sarah Shelton?"

"She's the producer of *Highlander, My Love*. She was at the games to scout filming locations. I may have offered her Blair Castle for a filming location for the show. Is that okay? She said they pay well."

Leith stared her. "Ye mean to tell me that these Americans want to film at Blair?"

"They might. I invited her and one of the show writers a chance to meet you and tour this place tomorrow." She held her phone and the business card tentatively, a look of uncertainty etched on her face. "Is that okay? If it is, I need to text her right away."

"It's more than okay, lass. It's brilliant." Leith grinned. "Ye're brilliant. Text her now so I can show ye how grateful I am."

Giggling, Ainsley quickly sent a text to Sarah, and then he pounced on her, carrying her to his bed where he planned to show Ainsley how grateful he truly was ... and how much he loved her.

AINSLEY WOKE TO THE SOUND OF WHISPERS IN THE dark. She pushed her blankets aside and stepped out of the bed, leaving Leith still sleeping. Her naked skin suddenly chilled, so she pulled on her underwear and pajamas before she searched for the source of the whispering that she had heard.

"Come with me." The voice drew her to the door almost as if she was in a dream.

"Come and see the stars..." the voice beckoned.

Ainsley followed the whisper out of the bedchamber and down the corridor. When she reached the top of the grand stairs that faced the castle's oak front door, she glimpsed a sliver of moonlight coming in from a high window. The beam of light formed the figure of a woman. She stood tall and slender, her pale blue gown a century old in fashion. Dark hair tumble down her back and was only held in place at the nape of her neck by a blue ribbon. She was beautiful and wild looking, which seemed fitting for a woman born in this beautiful, wild land. She beckoned to Ainsley, entreating her to follow as the door opened to the gravel drive beyond.

"Come and see your stars," the woman whispered.

Ainsley's feet carried her down the stairs to the doorway. The faint glimmer of the morning light seemed to pass right through the figure born of starlight and ancient magic, making the woman sparkle ever so faintly as she continued to walk toward the distant loch.

When Ainsley reached the water's edge, the woman raised a hand to the sky, where the stars still twinkled in defiance of the coming day.

"Yer stars are not crossed ... not like ours ... Don't turn away from the gift of what could be," the woman whispered. And then she vanished into the golden horizon, leaving Ainsley

standing barefoot on the shores of the loch. Goosebumps broke over her skin as she tried to figure out if she'd sleepwalked out to the loch or if she'd truly seen a ghost.

"Davina?" she breathed the name. The spirit, or perhaps nothing but a dream, had left Ainsley feeling a deep sense of peace.

"Is this the right thing to do, Gran? Is this what you want me to do?" Ainsley no longer felt silly speaking to the dead, because now she knew that they still had a voice, even if they only spoke to her in her dreams.

She held that last day of her grandmother's life in her mind, playing over the moment when the dear older woman still had been able to speak to her. Ainsley's grandmother had squeezed her hand, the pressure faint but persistent as she had spoken.

"Don't forget to live, Ainsley. Not just for me, but for yourself. Be brave."

Her gran's words had foreshadowed what Leith had said last night. Was Ainsley letting herself be ruled by fear? Davina hadn't let fear control her. She had lost the love of her life, but she had kept living. She had loved again. She had lived in a new country even after suffering a terrible loss and had made something of her life.

Just like I need to... Ainsley's eyes burned with tears. *Davina lost Daniel and came to America to start over. I lost Gran and I've come here ... I've come home.*

She watched a pair of ducks as they flew over the mountains and arced toward the loch before landing seamlessly in the water. The wave their landing created flowed outward before finally coming in toward the shore, toward her. Something deep moved inside Ainsley's heart, as if the earth itself had shifted, and she stood on new soil. Rather than feeling lost, she felt at home, finally, at long last.

She turned away from the loch to see Leith coming toward her. He had put on a t-shirt and a working kilt of dark blue and black plaid, as well as his boots. She loved it when he wore kilts. He carried a pair of coats over one arm. She hadn't even realized how cold it was out here; she'd been so lost in following Davina's ghost.

"Ainsley, lass, are ye all right?" He stopped by the water's edge with her and put one of the coats around her shoulders, helping her slide her arms into the sleeves. "I woke and ye were gone."

Ainsley reached up and trailed her fingertips over his cheek. She felt like she was seeing him clearly for the first time.

"I had the most peculiar dream," she confessed. "I saw Davina, or rather I think I saw her ghost. She led me here to see the stars." She pointed at the fading starlight. The golden sun illuminated Leith's face as he looked in the direction she pointed.

"I..." Ainsley suddenly felt too emotional to speak.

Leith wrapped his arms around her, holding her close as if they'd stood together in a thousand lifetimes.

"I want to stay here with you." She finally managed to get out the words that seemed to hold an entire universe within them. Leith's green eyes were as dark and alluring as the forests and hills on the mountains behind Blair Castle.

"If ye stay, then I will ask ye to marry me someday,

lass. I mean to be yer man for all of my days, if ye want me."

Her chest exploded with the sudden rush of heat and intense love for this man. He should be a stranger to her, yet he'd always been infinitely more from the moment she met him. When she'd been stranded on that road, weeping for losing Gran, he'd come into her life ... and she'd known that night there was something between them. She just hadn't known it would be the love of a lifetime.

"Someday..." She smiled up at him through happy tears. "When you ask, I'll say yes and I'll be yours for all of my days."

His eyes sparkled with mischief, and his kissable lips curved in that boyish grin that stole her breath. It was a grin that promised she'd always have laughter and love in her life.

"Then on that day, I'll stand here with ye and give ye my vows and my heart."

"My kilted groom," she chuckled. Then, she grasped him by the neck and pulled him toward her for a kiss that filled her heart with starlight and Highland magic.

THANK YOU SO MUCH FOR READING *THE KILTED GROOM*! Be sure to watch in my newsletter for a follow up sequel novella that it will be about the *Highlander, My Love* tv show writer who falls hard for the Scottish bad boy actor that plays the lead role!

· · ·

DON'T MISS ANY NEWS FROM ME! BE SURE TO follow me in more than one of the ways below:

TO LEARN MORE ABOUT MY BOOKS AND FOLLOW ME on social media and get new release updates be sure to visit my website at www.laurensmithbook s.com

ABOUT THE AUTHOR

Lauren Smith is an Oklahoma attorney by day, author by night who pens adventurous and edgy romance stories by the light of her smart phone flashlight app. She knew she was destined to be a romance writer when she attempted to re-write the entire *Titanic* movie just to save Jack from drowning. Connecting with readers by writing emotionally moving, realistic and sexy romances no matter what time period is her passion. She's won multiple awards in several romance subgenres including: New England Reader's Choice Awards, Greater Detroit BookSeller's Best Awards, and a Semi-Finalist award for the Mary Wollstonecraft Shelley Award.

To connect with Lauren, visit her at:
www.laurensmithbooks.com
lauren@Laurensmithbooks.com